Hello!

Ever feel like a fish out of water, or a pigeon in the middle of a flock of hawks?

I sure have. We moved around a lot when I was little, and I hated those first days at a new school. When I was a teenager, I moved overseas to Denmark and spent a year living on a farm there. Not only did I have to get used to a new house and a new school, I had to adjust to a whole new language!

At first I thought I'd never fit in. How could I make friends when I couldn't understand what anyone was saying? But after a couple of weeks, I could speak a few words in Danish. After a couple of months, I could talk about anything I wanted. I learned a lot about Denmark (the people there are so nice!) and I learned even more about myself.

When you find yourself in new surroundings, take it slow. Watch, listen, and learn from the people around you, but don't be afraid to be yourself. As long as you believe in yourself, you'll fit in anywhere.

Laurie Halse Anderson

Collect All the Vet Volunteers Books

LAURIE HALSE ANDERSON

VeT VOLUNTEERS

Time to Fly

PUFFIN BOOKS
An Imprint of Penguin Group (USA) Inc.

ACKNOWLEDGMENTS

Thanks to Kim Michels, D.V.M.; Lauren Powers, D.V.M., Diplomate
A.B.V.P. (Cavian Specialty); and Cathy East Dubowski.

PUFFIN BOOKS
Published by the Penguin Group
Penguin Young Readers Group, 345 Hudson Street, New York, New York 10014, U.S.A.
Penguin Group (Canada), 90 Eglinton Avenue East, Suite 700, Toronto, Ontario, Canada M4P 2Y3
(a division of Pearson Penguin Canada Inc.)
Penguin Books Ltd, 80 Strand, London WC2R 0RL, England
Penguin Ireland, 25 St Stephen's Green, Dublin 2, Ireland (a division of Penguin Books Ltd)
Penguin Group (Australia), 250 Camberwell Road, Camberwell, Victoria 3124, Australia
(a division of Pearson Australia Group Pty Ltd)
Penguin Books India Pvt Ltd, 11 Community Centre, Panchsheel Park, New Delhi - 110 017, India
Penguin Group (NZ), 67 Apollo Drive, Rosedale, Auckland 0632 New Zealand
(a division of Pearson New Zealand Ltd)
Penguin Books (South Africa) (Pty) Ltd, 24 Sturdee Avenue,
Rosebank, Johannesburg 2196, South Africa

Registered Offices: Penguin Books Ltd, 80 Strand, London WC2R 0RL, England

First published in the United States of America by Pleasant Company Publications, 2002
Published by Puffin Books, a division of Penguin Young Readers Group, 2009
This edition published by Puffin Books, a division of Penguin Young Readers Group, 2012

2 3 4 5 6 7 8 9 10

THE LIBRARY OF CONGRESS HAS CATALOGED THE PUFFIN EDITION AS FOLLOWS:
Anderson, Laurie Halse.
Time to fly / Laurie Halse Anderson.
p. cm.
Summary: Just when Zoe is starting to feel at home in Ambler, Pennsylvania,
living with her veterinarian grandmother and learning about a flock of wild parrots,
her actress mother arrives to take her to a new home in Los Angeles.
[1. Mothers and daughters—Fiction. 2. Grandmothers—Fiction. 3. Veterinarians—Fiction.
4. Parrots—Fiction. 5. Moving, Household—Fiction. 6. Ambler (Pa.)—Fiction.] I. Title.
PZ7.A54385Ti 2009
[Fic]—dc22 2009004862

Puffin Books ISBN 978-0-14-241224-4

Text set in JoannaMT
Designed by Jeanine Henderson
Printed in the United States of America

To Andrea Weiss, with thanks for everything

Chapter One

. . . .

"**D**irt! Dirt! Dirt! *Ugh!* Who *knew* there was so much dirt in the world?"

I brush my long hair back from my face and dip my scrub brush back into the bucket of soapy water. "I swear, it would be easier to just buy new kennels," I remark to my friend David Hutchinson, who's stuck with the same chore.

"You got that right," he says. He shakes his shaggy bangs out of his eyes and gazes off into the bright blue sky. "It's un-American not to be playing baseball on a day like this."

It is a gorgeous spring day. We ought to be doing something to enjoy it. But for some reason

Gran—otherwise known as Dr. J.J. MacKenzie, the best vet in Ambler—thinks it's the perfect day for cleaning. She's put all the Dr. Mac's Place volunteers to work—me, David, my cousin Maggie, plus Brenna Lake and Sunita Patel—giving the clinic a thorough cleaning from top to bottom. Windows, cabinets, closets, cages, kennels…she wants everything to sparkle.

Spring cleaning, Gran calls it. Good for the soul, she says. Here's Gran on spring. "A time of change, Zoe—when birds fly north with the warmer weather to build new homes. A time to wipe the slate clean and make a fresh start!"

Well, I've got spring fever all right—I'm itching to do *something*. But scrubbing kennels is definitely *not* what I had in mind.

Back home in New York, I never had to do much cleaning. I grew up in a high-rise apartment with my mom, and we had a wonderful housekeeper named Ethel, who mothered us and cooked and cleaned while my mother went off to work every day. Mom's an actress, and she had a regular part in a soap opera. Ethel kept the place so clean, I guess I never really knew just how dirty things could get.

In Manhattan, spring is a tulip struggling

up in a three-foot-square plot of dirt around a tree—a plot a hundred dogs will use for a pit stop before the day is over. Spring is millions of people pouring out onto the sidewalks, trying to catch the sun between the high-rises.

Mom and I had our own spring rituals: long walks in Central Park, shopping at Bloomingdale's for new spring clothes, buying fresh strawberries from the corner markets...Sometimes I really miss New York. And Mom.

"Kiiii-yaaaahhh!" David leaves the kennel-scrubbing to me and attacks some small area rugs hanging on a line for beating. His crazy, made-up karate moves make me laugh.

Sneakers, my black-and-brown mutt, thinks spring cleaning is a game. He barks at the rugs flapping on the line and tries to get us to play with him. Even Sherlock Holmes, Maggie's ancient basset hound, trots slowly around the yard in an unusual display of energy.

David finally collapses onto the grass. "That's it! I can't do any more. My honorable opponent has defeated me!"

I laugh and pull a small folded piece of paper out of my jeans pocket. Gran has been kind enough to make a To Do list so we won't run out of cleaning chores. Gee, thanks a lot, Gran. "Next chore on the list: 'Scrub the deck chairs.'" I announce.

Who knew anybody ever had to do that?

We're supposed to be cleaning the clinic, but I guess since I'm family, she decided to slip that home chore in on me. I glance over at the grimy furniture that's been sitting out through an entire Pennsylvania winter.

David groans as I grab him by the hand and pull him up to help. I start brushing off the dirt and dead leaves. "You want to help me with this?"

"Uh, I think I hear an energy bar calling me!" he answers, and sprints into the clinic. David is *always* hungry.

Well, at least this chore is outdoors, where I can enjoy the fine weather. A soft breeze flutters the new leaves on the big oak tree. Songbirds flock to our next-door neighbor's collection of bird feeders. I wish we could have a bird feeder in our yard, but Gran jokes that we've already got enough animals flocking to the clinic without advertising a free lunch. Besides, Socrates the cat would terrorize any bird that stopped for a snack. In fact, any bird in our yard would run a mortal risk of becoming Socrates' snack!

The birds flit between feeders. I see a flash of blue and look closer. A bluebird, maybe? They say it's good luck to spot the first bluebird of spring. I drop my brush and walk over to our neighbor's fence for a better view.

Wait a minute—that bird's not blue. Its head is blue, but its body is green. Besides, it's too big to be a bluebird. And its beak—

I peer closer. That's no bluebird. It's a parrot!

"David! Maggie!" I shout. "Come here—quick!"

Maggie comes running out of the house, her red ponytail bouncing; but by the time she gets here, the startled parrot has flown away.

"What's wrong?" Maggie cries, looking concerned. "Are you all right?"

"I'm fine—I just saw a wild parrot at Mr. Cowan's bird feeder!"

"Yeah, right." Maggie jams her hands on her hips and looks at me like I'm nuts. "Ha, ha, very funny."

"No joke," I insist. "It was green with a little blue cap—"

"And a little pink dress and black patent-leather shoes?" Maggie finishes. "Zoe, parrots don't fly around wild," she says in that I-know-more-about-animals-than-you-do voice she uses sometimes. "At least, not here in Ambler, Pennsylvania. Maybe in South America."

"But I saw it!" I insist.

"April Fools' Day was *last* week." Maggie smirks, then arches her eyebrows at me. "Are you trying to create a distraction to get out of cleaning? Give it up, Zoe. Even Houdini couldn't get out of doing spring chores for Gran." She flips her ponytail over her shoulder and turns to leave.

"Maggie, wait—I'm serious!" I say. "Maybe it'll come back—"

"I'm busy cleaning closets," she calls over her shoulder as she heads into the house. "Call me if you see an elephant or a chimpanzee."

Oooh—she's such a know-it-all sometimes! I grab a wet scrub brush and go to work on the deck chairs, taking out my frustration on the dirt.

When I first got here, a year ago, Maggie and I didn't exactly hit it off. Maggie has lived with Gran ever since she was a baby, when her parents were killed in a car accident. She was used to having Gran and the clinic all to herself. Right around the time I came into her life, Maggie started having trouble in school—and David, Sunita, and Brenna started helping out in the clinic. So both Maggie and I had to make some major adjustments in our lives, and it wasn't easy. But once we found we shared a real love for animals, things started to click between us. Now we know each other so well, it's almost scary—Maggie knows how to push all my buttons, and I can usually tell just what she's thinking. But annoying as she can be, it's still a really neat feeling to be that close to someone. I wouldn't trade it for the world.

I sit down on the steps of the deck and stare into the backyard next door. I should really keep scrubbing—I've got three more chairs to do after this—but I can't stop thinking about the parrot. Back in New York, there was this man who used to go jogging in Central Park with a big red macaw flying from tree to tree right behind him. I'm sure pet birds escape once in a while, just like any other pet. So why doesn't Maggie think that could have happened right here in Ambler?

It's true that Maggie knows a little more about animals than I do, having grown up with Gran. OK, I admit it—she knows a *lot* more. In New

York, I never had a pet, just an aquarium of saltwater fish. And sometimes my mom took me to see the animals at the Central Park Zoo. But Mom never wanted us to have pets. It seems kind of odd, considering her mother's a vet, but I guess not everyone's crazy about animals.

Maybe that has something to do with why Mom and Gran haven't been very close. I mean, I barely knew Gran when I arrived here last summer, after Mom lost her job. When the network canceled her soap, Mom took the opportunity to do something she's always wanted to do: go to California and try to break into movies. But she didn't want to bring me along. Our separation was supposed to last only a little while, but every "sure thing" Mom auditioned for fell through. So "a little while" turned into almost a year.

I went out to Los Angeles to visit Mom for Christmas. That was wonderful and awful at the same time. I mean, you're not supposed to *visit* your mom for holidays. It was frustrating, too. She had three callbacks while I was there, so we spent hours hanging out in waiting rooms for her turn to audition. At first it seemed exciting— what if she got the part?!—and we kept the boredom at bay by playing trivia games or quizzing each other with lines from our favorite movies. But when, one by one, Mom didn't get the parts, all the excitement went out of it. Mom summed it up: "Welcome to the glamorous world of acting."

Sometimes I wish my mom were a normal mom, the kind who makes home-cooked meals and checks your math homework. Brenna's, David's, and Sunita's moms are all like that, even though they have jobs, too. But then I think about how talented my mother is—about all the times she made her soap character seem so real, I almost forgot it was my mom there on the TV screen.

She used to tell me, "I don't want to spend my life sitting in some office somewhere, typing something nobody cares about till my fingers drop off." I can't argue with that. I know she's lucky to be doing something she really loves, even if it's a hit-and-miss kind of career. I just hate having her be a five-hour plane ride away. Too bad nobody makes movies in Ambler, Pennsylvania.

Something tugs at my sneakers. I look down. It's Sneakers, my dog. He's made living here a lot easier. I reach down to scratch behind his ears, but suddenly he runs to the edge of the deck and barks at the oak tree.

"Sneakers, what's gotten into you? Are you defending me against a tree?" I glance up—and catch a flash of blue between the green leaves.

"There it is again, Sneakers! I knew I didn't dream it!"

Chapter Two

. . . .

Of course, everyone else is inside, so nobody sees the parrot but Sneakers and me. And Socrates. He stares up at the tree too, his tail twitching.

The parrot flutters to a higher branch, then perches and looks down at me. He cocks his little round head first one way, than the other, as if sizing me up. Suddenly he lets out a loud "Brwaaaak! Phone home!"

I can't help giggling. The parrot is so cute. "Hey, bird, are you talking to me?" I call up to him.

"Pretty girl!" the parrot replies, bobbing up and down on the branch. Then he begins to preen his wings, just as though he wanted to make himself look nice for me. A green feather drifts to the ground.

I knew I was right—this is obviously an escaped pet parrot. Wait till I tell Maggie!

I pick up the feather and run inside, with Sneakers at my heels, as the parrot shrieks after me, "Pretty girl! Phone home!"

Gran is pouring milk to go with the brownies everyone's scarfing down.

"Guys, quick!" I shout. "There's a parrot in the backyard!"

"And I'm an Inca princess," Maggie says. "Have a brownie, Zoe."

"What's the matter with you?" I exclaim. "Don't you want to see it?"

"Sure, if it's got a pirate under it," David jokes.

"Look!" I say, holding up the green feather as evidence, like a lawyer in a courtroom.

Gran reaches for the feather. "Where did you find this?" she asks, suddenly interested.

"In—the—back—yard," I say slowly, as if they're all a bit dimwitted.

"It's beautiful," Sunita says.

Brenna frowns at the feather, puzzled. "But

it's the wrong color for any of the native birds around here."

"That's what I'm trying to tell you," I say. "It's not a native bird, it's a parrot. It even talks! It said 'Phone home,' just like E.T. in the movie."

Gran blinks. "It talked?"

"Yes!"

"Show me."

I shove through the screen door onto the deck with everyone crowding right behind me. But if the parrot is still in the tree, he's well hidden now. Avoiding the skeptical looks I know must be coming my way, I quickly scan the yard. Nothing. I check Mr. Cowan's bird feeders. Just ordinary birds. But what's that bright green spot on Mr. Cowan's lawn? "Look!" I whisper, pointing. "See?"

There he is, a bright green tropical bird like you'd see in a zoo or a pet shop, sitting loose in the middle of a very untropical Pennsylvania lawn. They can't miss him.

I slant Maggie an I-told-you-so look.

"Sorry," she whispers. "I believe you, I *believe you*!"

The parrot just sits there with his eyes half-closed, as if he's sleepy. Do parrots sleep on the ground? I don't know much about birds, but I would think parrots usually sleep in trees, where it's safe. I take a few steps closer. The parrot's beak opens and opens again, but no sound comes out, as if he's just too tired to get the squawks out. His feathers are all ruffled up, too. "He looks like a bright green feather duster," I whisper. "Gran, what do you think is wrong with him?"

"By the looks of him, he's either exhausted or sick," she replies.

"But he seemed fine when I saw him before," I say. "He was fluttering around in our oak tree. How could he get sick so fast? Do you think he fell?"

"Maybe some of the other birds attacked him because he looks so different. Maybe they know he's not from around here," David says.

"I don't think so," Gran says. "Let's see whether—"

Suddenly something low and orange streaks across the yard, straight toward the parrot. Socrates!

Before anyone else can even react, Sunita sprints to the fence and scoops Socrates into her arms. "Oh, no, you don't!" she tells him firmly, carrying him back into the house. Sunita is our resident cat expert—she's always one step ahead of the rest of us when it comes to reading a cat's mind. And Socrates, who treats the rest of us as if we were his personal servants, responds to Sunita as if she were a mystical cat charmer. (Is it just a cat thing? Or could Sunita teach me how to do that with Sneakers?)

As soon as Sunita gets Socrates inside, I start toward the sick parrot, but Gran stops me. "Wait, Zoe," she says in that soft but serious vet-to-the-rescue voice that we know to instantly obey. "Run and get me a towel, please."

I'm not sure what she wants it for, but I don't ask questions. I just race inside and grab a clean towel off the pile on the dryer, then zoom back out to the deck.

The parrot is still sitting on Mr. Cowan's lawn. I hand Gran the towel.

Gran strides across the yard, then eases through the side gate that leads into Mr. Cowan's yard, draping the towel over her right hand as she steals up behind the sick bird. She reminds me of Socrates stalking prey. Swiftly and silently she kneels down and captures the parrot in the towel. When she stands up, the towel is wrapped around the parrot, and Gran's fingers are around the bird's neck, immobilizing its head—I guess so it won't bite her. But the bird barely protests. Carefully supporting the lower half of the bird's body with her other hand, Gran walks briskly back to the clinic.

"Zoe, why don't you come help me with this bird," Gran calls over her shoulder. "The rest of you can go back to your chores." She heads for the Herriot Room, calling for Dr. Gabe.

I'm right behind her. "Doesn't it hurt the bird's neck to hold it like that?" My hand goes to my neck, and I swallow.

"Not at all," she assures me. "Birds have a very sturdy windpipe. But they don't have a diaphragm, like we do. A bird has to move its chest in and out to breathe. So if you hold it too tightly around its chest, you can suffocate it."

In the exam room, Gran cradles the parrot against her chest. "We need to rehydrate this fellow before we can do anything else," she says. "Sick birds are very vulnerable to dehydration. Let's start with a quick shot of fluids."

I've done this before. I go to the cabinet and get a syringe of lactated Ringer's solution. While Gran holds the parrot, Dr. Gabe slowly gives it an injection between the shoulders. I hate getting shots, but the bird doesn't even seem to feel it.

Watching the parrot up close, I notice that his head doesn't really look blue under the fluorescent lights. In fact, it's not blue at all, it's green, like the rest of him. "Gran!" I exclaim. "This isn't the parrot I saw before."

"What?" Gran looks puzzled. "Are you sure?"

I nod my head. "Positive. The talking parrot was about the same size and color as this one, but his head was blue, not green. And he seemed so alert and healthy. I mean, he was fluttering around in the oak tree, squawking and talking to me. He couldn't have gotten so sick this fast, could he?"

"It's not always easy to tell when a bird is sick," Dr. Gabe says. "In the wild, birds often hide any illness to protect themselves, because a sick bird is easy prey for predators. Unfortunately, pet birds tend to follow that same behavior pattern. That's why bird owners sometimes don't even notice something's wrong until their pet is really sick."

I shake my head. "But I'm *sure* this isn't the same bird."

"Well, we'll deal with that mystery later," Gran says, peering at the parrot, "after I take care of this little fellow."

"I'll get the oxygen cage," Dr. Gabe says.

"Is he that sick?" I ask.

"It's hard to know for sure, but he's certainly not doing too well," Gran replies. "Extra oxygen will help stabilize him and restore his breathing."

"Poor thing," I croon, reaching out a finger to stroke his bright green head.

Quickly Gran puts her hand on my arm. "It's best not to touch him, Zoe—not until we know what's wrong," she warns. "He might be contagious."

I jerk back my hand. "Really? People can catch bird diseases?"

"Yes, they can."

The bird has some junk around its eyes and beak. Ick—I don't want to catch *that*.

Dr. Gabe returns with a small plastic chamber. He sets it on the counter, plugs it in, then connects a thin tube to an oxygen tank. Gran tucks the parrot into the plastic chamber and closes the door.

I peek through the window. The box is heated, and the bird looks warm and cozy, still nestled in the towel. "How long does he stay in there?" I ask.

"A half hour should help him feel much

better," Gran says. "With some fluids in him and some oxygen, he'll be stronger, and it'll be easier for him to tolerate me handling him for the exam."

"Don't worry," I tell him through the window. "Gran's the best. She'll make you feel better soon."

But I can't help wondering about the other parrot with the pretty blue head, the one that talked to me. Can there really be *two* parrots flying loose around our neighborhood?

• • • • • • •

After half an hour, Dr. Gabe eases the parrot out of the oxygen cage. The bird looks a little more alert, but he still doesn't struggle much. Dr. Gabe holds the bird in a towel, the same way Gran did earlier.

He and Gran both have on surgical masks. Gran tells me to put one on, too, "just in case." A face mask makes me feel very official—but also a little anxious. If this bird has something serious, he might not make it.

"OK, Pickles," Gran says, nicknaming her small green patient. "Let's see what's bothering you."

I love watching Gran at work. She's focused but affectionate with her patients, calm and quick and gentle at the same time. Her hands move effortlessly, like a magician performing a trick that's been rehearsed a thousand times. And her face never gives away her thoughts. She keeps her feelings inside, so she won't frighten the animals—or their owners.

As Dr. Gabe holds Pickles in the towel, Gran begins by checking the bird's basic vital signs. She listens to his heart with a stethoscope and peers in his eyes with an ophthalmoscope. She parts the feathers on each side of his head to check his ears. (Yes, birds do have ears!) With the lightest touch she feels his neck, chest, and belly. Very gently she extends each wing and leg, one at a time.

Pickles looks frightened, but he doesn't struggle.

"Can you tell what's wrong?" I ask impatiently.

"Well, there's nothing obvious, like a broken bone," Gran replies. "But the nasal discharge and listless behavior tell us this bird is clearly not well. It could be a number of things. We'll just have to rule them out one by one. Can you grab me some cotton balls and alcohol, Zoe?"

While I get the supplies from the counter, Gran goes to a cabinet and comes back with a syringe. She wipes the bird's chest area with alcohol, then gives him an injection in the breast muscle.

"What's that?" I ask her.

"It's a broad-spectrum antibiotic," she says. "I want to get something into his system right away. Then, when we know what's wrong with him, we may switch to a more disease-specific medication." Gran looks up at Dr. Gabe. "What do you think, doc? Is our patient strong enough to give a blood sample?"

"I think he can handle it," Dr. Gabe replies. "The oxygen seems to have perked him up."

Carefully but firmly, Dr. Gabe tilts back Pickles's head. Through the small feathers I can barely see the pale skin of the neck that covers the bird's jugular vein.

"Alcohol," Gran says, and I hand her a soaked cotton ball. After cleansing the area, she slowly slips another needle into the vein and draws a thread of blood up into the syringe. Again,

Pickles doesn't react to the needle at all.

"Sterile cotton swab, please," she orders.

I open a fresh one, and she uses it to take a quick stool sample from the bird's hind end.

"That's it," Gran says. "You're all done, Pickles."

Pickles blinks at us. He looks woozy, the way I felt when I had the flu last January.

"Shall I prepare one of the small cages?" I ask.

"Yes," says Gran. "And I think we'd better quarantine him, just to be on the safe side."

"He has to stay all by himself?" I ask. "You think it's something that serious?"

"Well, we won't know till we get the tests back," Gran says. "But we don't know how long Pickles has been loose in the wild. He could have contracted psittacosis."

"Sit-a-what?"

She spells it for me. "It's a life-threatening disease. It's so contagious that most countries have strict import laws requiring exotic birds to be quarantined for more than a month when they first enter the country, to make sure they don't have it. It's often called parrot fever, but parrots can pass the disease on to other bird species, such as pigeons and poultry. They can even pass it on to humans."

Yikes. "You mean—Pickles could give it to us?"

Gran nods. "It's possible, although most healthy people can fight it off even if they're exposed. Still, we should be careful. Scrub up thoroughly before you leave, Zoe."

I fetch a small wire cage, line it with newspaper, and clip a water dispenser and a little feed bowl onto one side. Then I go to the sink and scrub my hands and arms all the way up to my elbows with lots of soap and hot water while Dr. Gabe puts the parrot into the cage, covers the cage with a towel, and carries it to the quarantine room.

Suddenly the back door to the clinic flies open, and Maggie rushes into the exam room. "You guys—there's a ton of…You won't believe—!" She pauses and gasps for air. "Come on—you've got to see this!"

Chapter Three

. . . .

We rush into the backyard. My mouth falls open as I gaze up into the oak tree. "Amazing!" I breathe.

Brightly colored parrots perch in the branches like ornaments on a Christmas tree. There must be dozens of them, in different sizes and different colors. Some perch where we can see them, as if showing off how beautiful they are. Others hide, their green feathers blending in behind the new spring leaves.

And the racket! I cover my ears. I bet people can hear this screeching and shrieking all over the neighborhood. Sneakers runs around yapping at the tree, as if he wants the parrots to come down and play.

"Brenna!" I gasp. "Do you have your camera?"

Brenna loves photography, and she's taken some awesome pictures of animals. Working at Dr. Mac's Place, she gets lots of opportunities for great animal shots, so she usually brings her camera with her.

"It's in my backpack!" She darts back inside to get it.

David has been trying to count the birds. "There's got to be at least fifty of them!" he exclaims.

"Gran," I ask, "where on earth did they come from?"

"I'm as bowled over as you are!" she says, running a hand through her short white hair. "Pet birds escape sometimes, but this is like a whole zoo got loose!"

I squint, looking for the friendly parrot with the blue head, the one who talked to me. "E.T...." I call softly. "There—that's him!" I point to a flash of blue and green that soars up out of the tree. "No, wait. His wings were different. They didn't look that long, and he flew in a more fluttery way."

"Maybe his wings were clipped," Gran says absently, studying the flock.

"People *clip* a bird's wings?" I ask, horrified.

"Just the long wing feathers," Gran explains. "It doesn't hurt the bird any more than a haircut hurts you. In fact, birds can often still fly even with clipped wings, especially if the feathers have started growing back. That's one way a pet bird can escape. Its owner takes it outside, thinking the clipped wings will keep the bird from flying, but the bird flies up into a tree and the owner can't catch it."

Brenna returns with her camera and starts snapping away. I'm glad we'll have pictures, because without them, none of the kids at school would believe this.

"What are we going to do, Gran?" Maggie asks.

"We could open our own zoo," David jokes. "One of those aviation—aviator—what do you call them?"

"Aviaries," Gran says. She sighs and shakes her head in wonder. It's not often that she's stumped. "I'm going to make some calls," she says, turning to go inside.

I grab her sleeve. "But what if these parrots

have the same sickness as Pickles? Shouldn't we try to catch them?"

Gran shakes her head. "You know how difficult it is just to catch a nervous pet bird that's flying around a closed exam room. To catch a flock of birds flying around wild would be next to impossible. Besides, they look healthy enough— at least, none of them appear to be as sick as Pickles. However, parrots do not just migrate to Pennsylvania. I'm going to make some inquiries to try and determine where these birds came from. Then we can decide what, if anything, to do about them. Meanwhile, you all"—Gran pauses to study the five of us—"need to finish your chores."

Everybody groans. I was hoping our exotic feathered visitors had made Gran forget something as dull and ordinary as chores. But she heads inside, and the others start to follow. Sunita grabs Socrates, and Maggie shoos the two dogs into the house.

I stare up into the tree. How are we supposed to think about scrubbing and cleaning with a miracle in our yard?

"Zo-eee," Maggie nags. "That means you, too."

"I'm cleaning the deck chairs," I remind her as I grab a brush and quickly start scrubbing a chair.

Maggie snorts and goes back inside to her closet cleaning.

At least I have a decent excuse to stay in the backyard. I want a little more time with these amazing birds.

Now that their audience has gone, the parrots become a little bolder and begin making forays into Mr. Cowan's yard. They look out of place perching at the bird feeders—almost comical in their clownlike colors, towering over the songbirds. The parrots flit back and forth from the oak tree to the feeders, squawking and fussing.

I look for the little blue-headed bird that talked to me, but I don't see him anywhere. I call out "Phone home!" a few times, but there's no reply.

I try to focus on my chair-cleaning task, but it's no use. My head is filled with questions about parrots. Quietly, I slide open the deck door and tiptoe inside, hoping nobody sees me. Fortunately, everyone seems to be busy in the clinic, cleaning. I sneak silently into the dining room, which has a floor-to-ceiling wall of books, and open volume P of Gran's trusty *Encyclopedia Britannica*. It's not a recent edition, but it includes a long article about parrots, enough to give me the basics.

The article says that parrots and their relatives live in many parts of the tropics. They eat mostly plants and fruit. They've been kept as pets for hundreds of years and are very intelligent, more so than most birds. In addition to their squawks, parrots use lots of body language to communicate.

I smile. That means that when the talking parrot bobbed his head at me, he was talking to me—in parrot language. I think he wants us to be friends!

I turn to the illustrated page showing all the different types of parrots. I've just identified the talking parrot as a blue-crowned conure when the phone rings.

Instead of answering it, I put the encyclopedia back and dart back out to the deck before I'm caught slacking off from my chore. A moment later, Maggie's head pops out of the clinic's back door. "Zoe—it's your mom!"

My heart skips a beat. Mom started calling

more often after Christmas, but then her calls tapered off. *So busy,* her quick scribbled postcards would always say. They always seem to include words like *almost, next audition, soon...*

I grab the phone. "Mom, hi! Listen, you won't believe what's going on." I start to tell her about the parrots, but she interrupts.

"Zoe, honey, are you sitting down?"

"Why?" I ask.

"Sit down!" she orders, sounding as if she's bursting with news.

"What, Mom? What?"

"Zoe—you can come *home*!"

Now I sit down. Actually, I stumble into a kitchen chair. "Home? We're going back to New York?"

At the sink, Maggie stares at me. She waves her arms at me and mouths, What? What?!

"I have a job!" Mom squeals into the phone. I hold the receiver out and rub my ear.

"Wow! I heard that!" Maggie says. She comes over and sticks her head next to the receiver, trying to listen in. I wave her away.

"I'm going prime time!" Mom announces proudly.

When I don't say anything, she adds, "I got the part!"

"What part?"

Mom laughs. "Honey, the part I…Zoe, I'm sure I wrote you about it. Didn't I? It's the lead female role on a new series they're shooting for next fall. I'll be playing a surgeon!"

Maybe she did mention this part. But I've been hearing this for a year—there have been so many auditions and promises—and everything always seems to fall through. So I've learned not to get my hopes up.

"When's the callback?" I ask.

"Sweetheart, it's a done deal. I've already got a contract!"

She sounds so thrilled, I start to get excited, too. My mother on prime-time TV!

"But—what about movies?" I sputter.

Mom laughs. "One thing at a time, sweetie. Just you wait, I'm on my way now. This is the big time, what I've been working for all these years."

"Oh, Mom, really?" I say, almost afraid to believe it. "There's no catch? You're not leaving something out?"

Something jingles across the phone lines.

I hazard a guess: "Uh, pocket change? You're working as a mime on the streets of L.A.?"

Mom laughs. "Oh, Zoe, don't be silly. It's keys!"

"Keys?"

"As in *house* keys. The keys to the house I just bought!"

"You bought a *house*?" I should be ecstatic. I should be screaming and jumping up and down. This is what I've been dreaming about for almost a year. Me and Mom—together. But instead I feel like I just got the wind knocked out of me.

When she left me at Gran's last summer, I felt like an unwanted kitten abandoned on a doorstep. And ever since, my heart's been on a roller-coaster ride. Every time Mom builds me up with her promises, things always seem to come crashing down. And now, just when I've finally started to feel at home here, out of the blue she tells me she's bought us a house.

A home? In *Southern California*?

Tears spring to my eyes out of nowhere. Maggie looks at me in alarm. I shake my head at her, as if to insist I'm OK.

"Well, it's not a *new* house, actually," Mom says with a laugh. "And it's not huge, but it's adorable, Zoe—just perfect for the two of us. Like one of the pictures you used to draw when you were little."

She remembers that? When I was little, Mom did all kinds of odd jobs while she was trying to get work as an actress, and we lived in a small fifth-floor walk-up apartment. At night she used to snuggle in bed with me and read me fairy tales. Then we'd talk about the little house we were going to live in one day. And sometimes I'd draw pictures of it, complete with a picket fence and a backyard with flowers and a dog. After she landed the role on the soap opera, we moved into a fancy high-rise with a doorman, and I guess I forgot about my pictures and our little fantasy home.

But apparently this house is no fantasy.

"It's got high ceilings and a front porch and a sweet little garden in the back," Mom continues, "so we can grow flowers and vegetables—"

Excuse me, vegetables? Mom's planning to grow *vegetables*? I've never seen her do gardening, not to mention cooking, in my life.

"—and it's in a terrific school district. You'll be going to Beverly Hills High! Isn't that wonderful?"

I gulp. Isn't that where those 902-whatever kids go?

Maggie points frantically at my arm, and I realize I've been twisting the phone cord around my wrist and my hand is starting to turn blue.

Slowly I untangle myself while Mom goes on and on. All about how there's this wonderful deli within walking distance. How we'll be so close to the beach. How maybe next year, if things go well, we could even put in a pool. "Practically everybody in L.A. has a pool, Zoe. You'll love it here!" I know she must be excited, but doesn't she realize I haven't said a word?

I should be as excited as Mom is. But I feel numb.

I'm going home. But home is Manhattan. Or now I guess it's Ambler, Pennsylvania.

"Well, I have to run, sweetie," Mom says hurriedly. "I'm due at the studio, and the traffic here is murder. Tomorrow I'm off for a few days, so I'll talk to Gran about the arrangements then."

"The arrangements?"

"Bye, honey! I love you!" She blows me a kiss over the phone, and then she's gone. The dial tone hums in my ear.

I hang up the phone and just stare at the floor.

"Zoe?" Maggie says. "What's going on?"

I glance up at my cousin—a cousin I barely knew a year ago. A cousin who's as different from me as a dog is from a cat. A cousin who's ...like the sister I never had.

"Mom got a job," I tell her. "I guess I'm going home."

Maggie's mouth drops open. "You're going back to New York?"

I shake my head. "To L.A."

"L.A.?" she exclaims. "But that's not your home! You stayed there for, what—five whole days at Christmas?" She kicks at the leg of the kitchen table with the scuffed toe of her sneaker.

What's she so mad about? I'm the one who has to go, not her.

Maggie glares at the floor. "If any place is your home, it's here with us."

She glances up at me, and a scared look passes between us. We've had our rough times. She had trouble sharing Gran with me when I first came, because Gran's the only mom she's ever known. But we've been through a lot together since then. Maggie's problems with school...my trouble training Sneakers...sharing a bathroom (she says I'm prissy; I say she's a slob). We cried together when Gran's friend Jane lost her dog Yum-Yum to cancer. And we both understand what it's like not to have a complete set of parents.

"Come on," she says roughly. "Let's see if Gran has any news about those crazy parrots." It's like I can read her mind—she's breaking up the scene before it gets too mushy.

I follow Maggie into the clinic, but my thoughts are a thousand miles away. Three thousand miles, to be exact—the distance between Ambler and Los Angeles.

A real home of our own...Mom and I have never had that. At least, we've never had a house. But isn't a home more than that? Gradually I become aware of a dull, sad ache in my stomach. It's like homesickness—the same sensation I had when I first arrived here. Except this time, it's the thought of leaving here that hurts.

Chapter Four

· · · · · · · · · · · ·

We have no time to chat about the phone call. Gran has plans of her own. "We're taking a little field trip," she announces.

"Yes!" David pumps his fist in the air. He loves animals—especially horses—but cleanup chores aren't his favorite part of working at Dr. Mac's Place.

"Where are we going?" Sunita asks.

"To the zoo," Gran explains.

Now we all cheer. A zoo trip beats chores any day.

Dr. Gabe stays behind to see patients.

"Keep an eye out for E.T.," I tell him. "If you

hear a parrot talking in the yard, that's him. Try to get him to stay in the yard until I get back."

"Well, I'll be pretty busy minding the clinic," says Dr. Gabe, laughing. "But I'll do my best, Zoe."

Brenna, David, Sunita, Maggie, and I pile into the van. "We're going to visit a friend of mine who's an expert on parrots," Gran tells us. "Maybe she'll have some ideas about the flock that's taken over our oak tree."

When we get to the zoo, we head past the monkeys, past the lions and tigers, straight to the bird house. As we near the building, Gran calls out, "Tasha!"

"J.J.!" A tall woman a little younger than Gran turns around and smiles at us. Her curly brown hair is touched by gray, and her green eyes are warm. She strides forward and gives Gran a hug. "It's so good to see you."

Gran turns to us. "This is Dr. Tasha Timmons, a good friend of mine. She's my brain trust when I've got bird questions."

We introduce ourselves, and then Dr. Timmons leads us into the aviary for a tour.

First we go through a set of large double doors into an alcove. After those doors close, we pass through another set of double doors into a huge room with a glass ceiling. It's like stepping into a jungle. We're surrounded by lush tropical trees, vines, and flowers. There's even a small waterfall. The air is so steamy and warm, I pull off my sweater and tie it around my waist. The zoo workers are better dressed for this tropical weather in uniforms of khaki shorts and green polo shirts.

"Come on, this way," Dr. Timmons says.

We follow her along a path that winds around through the jungle. Colorful birds perch in trees above us, chirping and cawing and shrieking. The sound is wild and almost spooky. I've heard bird calls like this on nature programs, but here it's the real thing.

David ducks as a long-legged bird swoops across the path. "It sounds like a Tarzan movie in here," he says. "Why are the birds making so much noise?"

"Like most birds, parrots are very social, vocal animals," Dr. Timmons explains. "They're smart, too. As you probably know, with training some parrots can learn to say hundreds of words."

"One of the parrots in our wild flock speaks English," I tell her. "I call him E.T. because he says 'Phone home.' We figure he's an escaped pet."

"Or an abandoned one," says Dr. Timmons.

Sunita shakes her head. "Why would anybody just dump a pet parrot?"

"Yeah, aren't they expensive?" David asks.

"They are. Even so, some people become smitten with the *idea* of having a pet parrot and buy one on impulse, without learning about the reality of parrot ownership first," Dr. Timmons says. "Parrots tend to be feisty, and without daily attention they get bored and develop bad habits like biting. Their powerful beaks can bite hard enough to crack a nut, so a nippy parrot isn't something you want around the house." Dr. Timmons pauses to point out two large parrots high in a tree. "Scarlet macaws, a mating pair. The female is new to our zoo, so we're delighted she's already paired up with our male."

We crane our necks and gaze up at the majestic red-and-yellow birds. I think I saw one or two in the oak tree that looked similar to these.

"As David noticed, parrots make a lot of noise, more than some people can tolerate," Dr. Timmons continues. "And some parrots can live fifty years or more, so that's a lot of squawking!

Unfortunately, sometimes when people decide they don't want their pet anymore, they just let it loose outside rather than making the effort to find it a new home."

"That's so irresponsible!" Maggie snorts.

"And cruel!" I add. We know it happens—all too often. We see plenty of abandoned pets at Dr. Mac's Place. People often buy their kids or their friends pets as gifts at Christmas or Easter without thinking it through or finding out what kind of care the pet requires. Then the owners decide they don't want the pet anymore. Some people even think it's a kindness to set a pet free.

"It *is* cruel," Dr. Timmons agrees. "Virtually all pet parrots are hatched and raised in captivity, and in order to socialize them, they're hand-fed by humans from day one. They don't have survival skills, and their odds of surviving for very long in the wild are slim. I hope you can catch E.T. and find his owners, or at least find a good home for him."

With a glance at Gran, I nod solemnly at Dr. Timmons and make up my mind right then and there: no matter what, I'm going to find a way to capture E.T. and get him home, wherever that may be for him.

After our walk through the aviary, Dr. Timmons treats us to a quick tour through the zoo's veterinary hospital. It's huge, a lot bigger than Gran's clinic. The vets here have to take care of all kinds of animals, from gorillas and giraffes to tarantulas and naked mole rats, and everything in between.

"Wouldn't this be a cool place to work?" Maggie murmurs to me.

I nod in agreement. It sure would! (Well, except for the tarantulas.)

As Dr. Timmons takes us through some of the operating rooms, Gran brings up the parrot flock.

"I wonder where they came from," Dr. Timmons muses. She turns to me. "Do they all talk?"

"No, not that I've heard," I answer. "The ones in the flock act sort of wild compared to E.T. He looks right at me, but the parrots in the flock are more skittish and shy, like the birds you have here."

"They sound more like wild parrots, then," says Dr. Timmons.

"But why would wild parrots be flying around loose here in Ambler?" asks Brenna. "They're certainly not native to this area!" Brenna's parents are wildlife rehabilitators. They have a special license that allows them to care for wild animals that are injured or sick. Last winter her family even had an orphaned fawn recuperating in their backyard. Brenna knows a lot about wild animals. Of course, even I know that wild parrots don't live in Pennsylvania. Or didn't until now.

"It's possible these parrots escaped from a breeder," says Dr. Timmons.

Gran nods. "That thought occurred to me, too. I did place a call to the sheriff, just to see if anyone had reported a breakout of parrots. But he hadn't heard anything. He said he'd call back if he did."

"Maybe the parrots were freed by animal rights people," David suggests. Maggie rolls her eyes, like it's a dumb thing to say, and swats David on the shoulder. "Well, they could have been! You don't know!" David says indignantly, swatting her back.

Ignoring their squabbling, I turn to Dr. Timmons. "Is there anything we can do to help the parrots?"

"They're probably better equipped to survive

on their own than a tame, hand-fed bird," she replies. "In fact, I'd say your E.T. is lucky he hooked up with them—they should be able to lead him to food and help him avoid predators. Being part of a flock is a protective measure for birds," she adds. "Still, the parrots may need people to help provide food, especially in the winter, when everything's dead and snow covered. Even if they're able to keep warm, getting enough to eat will be a problem for them."

A zoo staffer calls Dr. Timmons into an office. She excuses herself as we thank her for the tour.

On our way out, we pass a young man who is examining a big bird with a huge beak. It has to be a toucan. I realize with embarrassment that I recognize the bird from the box of Froot Loops cereal that Maggie eats! I can't help pausing to watch. The toucan lies quietly on an examining table.

"Is that toucan sedated?" I ask the man.

"She is. Had to put that big beak out of commission long enough for me to treat her." The veterinarian turns to me, and his face breaks into a smile. "Say, you look a little young to be a vet student, but you sound like you know your way around animals."

Gran nods proudly. "My granddaughter here is quite an animal lover. We might make a vet out of her yet."

Zoe Hopkins, D.V.M. That has a nice ring to it. I grin, imagining what Mom would say if I told her I wanted to be a vet like Gran. She'd probably faint.

Mom. With all the excitement over the parrots, I've been able to avoid thinking about her phone call. Now it all comes rushing back—the thought of leaving Gran and Maggie and Dr. Mac's Place, moving to California...My grin fades and I turn away, swallowing a stupid lump that suddenly swells in my throat.

Gran lays a gentle hand on my shoulder. "Zoe? Are you all right?"

I meet her gaze briefly. With her sharp blue eyes, she's searching my face in a way that reminds me of how she studies her animal patients, looking for clues to their illness or injury. But the confusion I'm feeling isn't something you can see with the eye, or even with an X-ray. It isn't something you can solve with a splint or a shot or a pill. I shrug and look away again. Does

Gran know what my mother is planning? Does she think it's for the best?

• • • • • • •

Gran drops the other kids off at their homes. As soon as we're back at the clinic, I rush to the backyard to check on the parrots, but the oak tree is empty. Only a few cardinals take turns swooping down to Mr. Cowan's feeders.

I suppose it was silly of me to think the parrots would be waiting for us. Yet somehow I was hoping that they'd know we care about them, that this is a safe place.

"They're gone!" I shout, shoving through the back door into the kitchen.

"Shhhh!" Maggie hisses, with the phone to her ear. "I'm ordering pizza!"

"Pizza?" I ask Gran.

Gran pretends to shrug helplessly. She's been on an anti-takeout campaign lately, but it looks like Maggie won this round. "I made her promise to order at least one vegetable," Gran says with a laugh.

"Do olives count as a vegetable?" Maggie asks.

Gran sighs. "How about green pepper—or even broccoli if they have it?"

Maggie makes a face, then asks into the phone, "What else have you got in the vegetable department?"

I laugh and pull open the refrigerator door. "I'll make a salad."

"That would be lovely, Zoe," Gran says. She opens a cupboard and sets out plates and salad bowls.

I dig out the lettuce and an assortment of raw veggies. Before I came, most of the meals Gran and Maggie ate were canned, frozen, or delivered. Gran's too busy to cook, and Maggie leans toward artificial colors and flavors, so she didn't mind just opening a box for dinner.

That's one way my mom is like her mother: she never cooks. Luckily for me, Ethel loved to cook, and she taught me how. We even used to watch the food channel together...*Don't think about New York, or Ethel, or Mom right now.*

"Gran, do you think the parrots are OK?" I ask as we tear the romaine for salad. I think of the lush jungle in the aviary. "What if they can't find enough to eat?"

"You'd be surprised how tough these birds can be," Gran replies. "There are flocks of parrots living wild in many parts of the U.S.

There's even a flock of Monk parakeets living wild in Chicago."

"Parakeets? Those cute little birds you see in pet shops?"

"No. The Monk, also known as the Quaker parakeet, is actually a type of small parrot. No relation to those little pet-store budgies, even though they're both called parakeets," Gran explains.

"Isn't Chicago even colder than Pennsylvania in the winter?" I ask, and Gran nods. "So what do the people there do about the Monk parakeets?"

"As far as I know, the birds manage to survive more or less on their own." Gran comes over to help me slice radishes. "Monk parakeets are unique among parrots because they build nests—huge ones—and that probably helps them keep warm through the winter," she adds. "Some biologists and bird watchers are keeping track of the flock and trying to protect the Monks, which I'm afraid have a bad reputation. Monk parakeets are thought to cause crop damage in Argentina, where they're native, so there's been concern that the same thing might happen here in the U.S., too."

I frown. How could a measly little flock of

parrots cause more crop damage than, say, a herd of deer, or even a big flock of crows? "Have wild parrots damaged any crops in the U.S.?" I ask Gran.

"So far there's no evidence of it," Gran says. "Still, in many states—including Pennsylvania—it's illegal to own a Monk parakeet for that very reason: the government is afraid that pet birds will get loose, naturalize into wild flocks, and then damage farm crops. If you're caught owning a Monk, the law requires the bird to be euthanized—put to sleep."

The doorbell rings, and Gran and Maggie go to get the pizza. As I toss the salad, it occurs to me that maybe we could do the same thing right here in Ambler that the biologists in Chicago are doing. We could set up a network of people to keep track of how the parrots are doing and make sure nobody tries to hurt them. Sunita could even help me put up a Web site for people to post their sightings of the Ambler parrots, so we can find out where they're roosting. We already know one of those places is Gran's oak tree, but there've got to be others.

My mind starts going a mile a minute, planning out a parrot-protection strategy. We could send some of Brenna's photos to the *Ambler Sentinel* and see if they'll send a journalist over to do a story on the parrots, to educate the public about them. In the fall, maybe we could get some pet stores to do promotions to encourage people to put out food for the parrots over the winter…

And then it comes back to me: I may not even be here in the fall.

· · · · · · ·

That night in bed, I can't seem to fall asleep. Watching the curtains move in the warm spring breeze, I can smell spring. The narcissus bulbs we planted last fall by the clinic's small parking lot are blooming like crazy; their smell perfumes the whole front yard and wafts up through my window. And I smell something else—the rich green smell of the earth coming back to life. New York never smelled like this at night. I wonder, what do L.A. nights smell like—car exhaust fumes? How can people there enjoy spring when they never have winter?

A scene from one of my favorite movies, *The Wizard of Oz,* pops into my head. Mom and I must have watched it a thousand times. It's that scene where Dorothy closes her eyes, clicks her ruby slippers together, and murmurs over and over, "There's no place like home, there's no place like home," as she waits for the magic to take her home where she belongs.

But where do I belong? Where's my home? I don't even know anymore.

As I drift off to sleep, an owl hoots in the distance, a lonely sound. And then I think I hear another sound, so far away I'm not even sure if it's real or I'm dreaming: the distant squawk of a parrot. This place isn't the parrots' real home, either. But I want to help them feel at home here in Ambler—just as I do.

Chapter Five

• • • • • • • • • • •

Sunday morning I wake up late and stretch in the sunlight like a contented cat. Sneakers yaps when he hears me stirring and leaps onto my stomach.

"Sneakers!" I shriek, grabbing him as I sit up, glad he's just a lightweight mutt and not a heavy husky or Saint Bernard. He licks my face like a lollipop, and I hug him tight, laughing.

After all the confusing thoughts swirling through my mind yesterday, I suddenly feel clearheaded. Maybe a good night's sleep was all I needed.

I know what the acting business is like. One

day you're a star—and the next day you're a waitress again. I've been there with Mom before. Sure, she sounded certain yesterday, but my mother's a romantic, an eternal optimist. She looks for sunshine even when the weather station predicts rain. That's one of the reasons we had so much fun all those years she was raising me alone.

I like to dream, too, but I also like to keep my feet on the ground. And right now, my feet are firmly planted *here*. I'm all settled into my life with Gran and Maggie and Sneakers and all the other animals that are part of our lives—which now includes a bunch of parrots who need my help.

I kiss Sneakers, dress, brush my hair, and fly downstairs.

At the kitchen table, Maggie is dribbling pink milk onto the sports pages as she slurps up her Froot Loops.

"So, what are we doing today?" I ask cheerfully. "Painting the clinic? Nailing on a new roof?"

Maggie glares at me. "Don't give Gran any ideas."

"Maggie, you're drooling. Yuck! Don't talk with your mouth full!"

"Who are you, my mother? Don't tell me what to do."

As she speaks, a spray of milk flies out of her mouth. We look at each other and giggle hysterically.

Just for fun I peer into her bowl of multicolored sugar and chemicals, and gasp. "I think I saw that cereal in yesterday's newspaper!"

Maggie freezes with the spoon in her mouth. "Huh?"

"Yeah—the headline said, 'Toxic Cereal Turns Seventh-Grade Girl's Freckles Purple.'"

"Very funny," Maggie retorts. "I'll have you know this cereal is fortified with 10 essential vitamins and minerals."

"Don't you get it?" I counter. "If it had healthy ingredients in it in the first place, they wouldn't have to fortify it."

Maggie refuses to dignify my comment with a reply—or maybe she just can't think of anything to say. Feeling smug, I set about making my own breakfast—sliced strawberries on yogurt, a toasted English muffin with honey, and orange juice.

Maggie's lowered the volume on her slurping now that she's lost in the sports pages. Sherlock and Sneakers sleep by our feet beneath the table. Socrates dozes in a patch of sunlight on the wide windowsill by the table. And I can hear some Mozart coming from the clinic—Gran enjoying her "morning off" by doing what she loves best, checking on her animals. Everything feels cozy and peaceful.

And I'm a part of it all. I work in the clinic, I help care for the animals, I cook and make sure Gran and Maggie don't die of malnutrition. Sneakers and I even visit hospitals to cheer up the patients.

In New York I never felt needed. As much as Mom loves me, I sometimes got the feeling I was a burden to her. After all, without me she wouldn't have had to hire Ethel, who must have been expensive. And I guess Mom sort of confirmed that feeling when she went off without me to pursue a Hollywood career.

But here, I'm needed and wanted—and that's such a good feeling. Will I have that feeling living in Los Angeles with Mom? Or will I just feel like a burden again?

Maggie kicks me under the table.

I glance up. "What?"

Maggie stares at me like I'm a dope. "Hello!

If you don't get Sneakers outside, he's going to pee."

One look at my dog tells me Maggie is right. Sneakers is pacing back and forth by the back door, watching me with his I-have-to-go-*now* look. When he catches my eye, his tail wags hopefully.

"Oops," I mutter, ignoring Maggie's self-satisfied smirk, and scoot out the back door with Sneakers before he gives me something to clean up besides breakfast dishes.

While Sneakers relieves himself beside the oak tree, I search the branches. But the familiar morning bird song, unbroken by squawks or screeches, has already told me the parrots aren't here.

A screen door slams and our next-door neighbor, Mr. Cowan, comes out carrying a tray.

"Hi, Mr. Cowan!" I call.

"Good morning, Zoe," he says, coming over to the end of his deck. "Nice morning for bird-watching."

"Did you see what we saw yesterday?" I ask.

"The parrots?" He nods. "Sure did. I've been checking the news to see if anybody's figured out how they got here, but so far nobody seems to know."

He rests his tray on the railing of his deck, and I notice what's on it—oranges. *Lots* of oranges. Enough to feed a whole family for a week.

Mr. Cowan follows my gaze. "These are for the parrots, in case they come back. Birdseed isn't really the best diet for parrots. They prefer fruit and vegetables." He picks up a knife and begins slicing the oranges. "Want to help?"

"Sure. I'll be right over." I let Sneakers back inside, then join Mr. Cowan on his deck and start slicing up oranges while he spreads the slices on the railing of his deck. Mmm. The oranges smell sweet and sunny and make my mouth water.

"Go ahead, help yourself," Mr. Cowan says with a smile. "The birds won't miss a slice or two."

Mr. Cowan is a retired university professor, a botanist, so I guess that makes him Dr. Cowan, but nobody calls him that. He's the sweetest man you'll ever meet, but I think he's lonely. His wife died about two years ago, Gran told me. He loves to garden. Last summer he put in a little pond with lily pads and a fountain and these giant goldfish called koi in it. He has a small rose garden, a big vegetable garden, and about a dozen kinds of bird feeders all over his yard.

Maybe I can enlist Mr. Cowan to serve on the front lines of my parrot-protection program. He's obviously a big-time bird lover, and he knows something about parrots to boot. I decided to feel him out. "Maybe with our help, the parrots will stay and make their home right here in Ambler."

"They're delightful creatures, indeed. But you know, Zoe, there's more to think about than just the parrots' survival." He opens a large plastic tub and begins refilling the feeders on the deck with regular birdseed. "There's also the impact on the local environment."

"You mean like causing crop damage?"

"I mean any kind of impact. It's always a risk when a foreign bird or animal or even plant invades a new environment," Mr. Cowan explains. "There's no way to know for sure how the foreigner will affect native plants and animals. Foreign species can carry diseases and parasites that the native species have no defenses against."

I nod, thinking of Pickles. Could he have infected other birds with his sickness before we took him into the clinic?

Mr. Cowan continues. "Sometimes foreign

invaders simply out-compete the native species for food and habitat." He clips the plastic cover back on the seed bin and eases himself into a chair, warming to his topic. I can just imagine him lecturing to a class. I'll bet he was a good teacher. "Look at foreign species like the lamprey eel and the zebra mussel, which as a result of ocean ship traffic have moved into the Great Lakes. As their populations have grown, the native fish and shellfish populations have declined."

"So you really think this parrot flock might grow and crowd out our native birds?" I look around at the chickadees and sparrows clustered at the feeders. They may not be as showy as the parrots, but I certainly wouldn't want them to be driven away from their own food and nesting places.

He shrugs. "I'm not saying it's likely to happen, but it's a possibility that shouldn't be ignored." He pauses, then adds, "Still, now that they're here, one feels a certain responsibility toward them. Almost as if they're guests at our table." He smiles, his eyes crinkling at the corners. "I can't see just letting them go hungry."

He stands up and takes the tray, and I wave

good-bye as I head across the yard back to Gran's, my head spinning. The more I learn about these parrots, the more complicated and confusing everything becomes.

In the kitchen, Gran has joined Maggie at the breakfast table. "Good news," Gran says as I walk in the back door. "The lab just called to say that Pickles does not have psittacosis."

That's a relief, especially after what Mr. Cowan was saying. "So what *does* he have?"

"Probably just an upper-respiratory infection. I'll keep him in quarantine for six more weeks to make sure he's no longer contagious, and I'll continue the antibiotics, too, in case he's got a bacterial infection."

"What about E.T.?" I ask. "Do you think he could have become infected with whatever Pickles has?"

"It's possible. It certainly won't hurt to keep an eye on him," Gran says.

How can I keep an eye on him if he won't stick around? What if E.T. gets as sick as Pickles while he's somewhere else, and he dies because nobody is there to help him? "Gran, I think we should try to catch him."

"Easier said than done, Zoe." Gran takes a sip of her coffee.

"I know, but if he was someone's pet, then he's used to having someone take care of him." I think about how E.T. spoke right to me. "In fact, I think he *wants* someone to take care of him."

Someone like me, perhaps.

Sneakers is pawing his water bowl, so I take it to the sink to fill it. "Gran, could *we* keep him?"

"Keep who?" Maggie asks.

"E.T. He's so smart—you should hear him talk. Maybe we could teach him to answer the phone: 'Bwaack, Dr. Mac's Place!' Wouldn't that be cute?"

"Let's not get ahead of ourselves," Gran says as she rises from the table. "Zoe, I appreciate your feelings, and I admire your desire to help E.T. But although I may know a little about treating sick birds, I am not experienced at owning parrots. And neither are you."

"But Gran, everybody has to start somewhere!" I point out. "How am I supposed to get experienced?"

Gran shakes her head. "Zoe, we already have

too many animals as it is. Besides," she goes on, "how would you feel if he was your pet who was missing? Wouldn't you want him back? Why don't you check the classified ads in the newspaper and see if anyone's looking for a missing parrot."

Trying to think of an argument, I hoist up the bag of dog food to fill Sneakers's bowl. It's so annoying when Gran's right all the time. Before I can think of a good reply, the front door swings open. When I see who's standing there, I drop the entire bag of dog food on the floor. Sneakers bounds over and starts wolfing up the spilled food, but nobody scolds him. Even Gran and Maggie are speechless.

"Surprise!"

You can say that again.

It's my mother.

Chapter Six

. . . .

I don't know whether to laugh or cry. I rush into my mother's arms and do a little of both.

Mom drops her bags and hugs me. "Zoe, sweetheart! Oh my gosh, you're almost as tall as I am." She steps back and holds me at arm's length, then squeezes me again. "You're growing up so fast!"

With a sharp bark, Sneakers runs over to make sure this intruder isn't hurting me. I guess he can tell I'm OK, more or less, because his tail starts wagging and he jumps up on Mom, getting her white pants muddy. Not a great start to their relationship.

I untangle myself from Mom and scoop Sneakers into my arms. "Chill," I whisper in his ear. "She's not an animal person."

"Well, this is a surprise," Gran says at last.

"What, not happy to see me?" Mom shoots back as she pulls Maggie into an awkward hug.

My usually sassy cousin is still speechless—a first for her. I guess she's never seen a TV actress up close before.

"Oh, Rose, of course I am," Gran says. "We just weren't expecting you, that's all. How'd you get here?"

"Well, I was so excited when I got off the phone with Zoe yesterday that as soon as our rehearsal was done, I jumped on a red-eye flight straight to Philadelphia," she says, beaming at me.

She sure looks good for someone who slept in an airplane seat all night. In fact, she looks better than ever—and so much happier than when I saw her at Christmas. I guess life in the fast lane agrees with her.

"You should have called!" Gran says. "We could have met you at the airport."

Mom waves that notion away as if it hadn't occurred to her. "You know how impulsive I am, Ma."

"That I do, Rose. Impulsive—and determined."
Gran gives Mom a quick hug.

I watch Mom and Gran carefully. I never
thought they looked much alike, but now, seeing
them together, I can spot the similarity in the
way they hold themselves—with a certain inner
poise and confidence, as if they know where
they belong in the world.

I wish I did.

Suddenly the bell to the clinic rings. Clients
have arrived.

Mom raises a perfectly plucked eyebrow. "On
Sunday, Ma?"

Gran shrugs. "The world has changed since
you were a girl, Rose," Gran says. "The clinic
is usually open all weekend and several nights a
week."

"Don't you get tired ot it?"

"Do you get tired of acting?"

Mom grins sheepishly. "Touché. Need a
hand?"

Gran hooks her arm through my mom's and
leads her toward the clinic door. "I can always
use another pair of hands."

I snort. "*You* help in the clinic? No offense,
Mom, but you can't even stand the smell of a

sour washcloth. This place is filled with disgust-ing smells, trust me."

Mom lifts her chin and gazes down her nose at me, looking like a younger version of Gran (except with more makeup and an expensive haircut). "You don't think I know my way around a veterinary clinic?"

"No," I fight to keep the smirk off my face.

"Hmph! You forgot one thing, Zoe—I grew up here. This was my home." Mom unbuttons the cuffs of her black shirt and neatly rolls them up above her elbows. She glances down at her white pants, now soiled with doggy paw prints, courtesy of Sneakers. "Well, your dog must have known what was in store for me. No need for me to change at all—I'll just wash everything tonight." She turns to Gran. "Dr. MacKenzie, I am at your service. Again."

Gran is the one laughing now—at me—as the three of us head into the clinic.

"Are you coming, Maggie?" I ask her.

"Um, I told David I'd go and shoot baskets with him," she says, and escapes out the front door.

I shrug and follow Mom into the clinic. This I can't miss.

Apparently people have been spotting the parrots all over town, and the clinic waiting room is abuzz.

"I saw them in the park behind the bank just yesterday!"

"Aren't they colorful? And there's so many of them. I wouldn't have believed it if I hadn't seen it with my own eyes!"

"A flock of parrots, right here in Ambler. Imagine!"

Our clients seem almost as excited about the parrots as I am. If I printed up some flyers about what kinds of food the parrots like to eat, I'll bet our clients would be glad to help out in my parrot-protection program.

In the Dolittle Room, I find Mom sitting on a high stool, talking to a teenage girl holding an adorable puppy with huge brown eyes and long, curly reddish fur. "I got Shirley at the Humane Society," the girl is saying. "We think she's a terrier-spaniel mix."

Gran strokes the puppy's curly coat. "Could be some poodle in there, too. She's a cute little thing, whatever she is." Gran checks her clipboard. "Looks like she had her shots before she left the Humane Society. What can we do for her today?"

"Could you just check her over, and then show me how to clip her nails?" the girl asks. "My dad says I can't keep her unless she's healthy and I can groom her myself."

Gran smiles and nods. "Rose, why don't you show Lauren how to clip Shirley's nails. I'll be back to do the physical in ten minutes," Gran says.

I come to Mom's rescue. "It's all right, Gran. I'll show her how to—"

Mom holds up her hand. "I'll be glad to give your pup a pedicure, Lauren." Mom takes the clippers from the drawer of the exam table and reaches for a paw. I bite my lip, hoping Mom knows what the heck she's doing. She seems awfully confident—but then she's a skilled actress, trained to play whatever part she finds herself in as if born to the role.

"Zoe, why don't you hold Shirley while I show Lauren the technique," Mom suggests.

The puppy gives my cheek a quick lick— sweet puppy breath!—as I settle her in the crook of my left arm. I rest my other hand on her fat, fuzzy tummy to hold her steady. Shirley looks up at me with her trusting brown eyes, and I can't help but smile down at her. I think I'm in love. Lucky Lauren.

Mom selects a paw and brings the clippers to the nail. "Just be careful not to clip off too much," she instructs Lauren, who watches closely. "This pink part down here is called the *quick*. You don't want to clip it, or it will bleed and hurt her. Right now her nails aren't very long, so it's a little tricky. But each time you clip them, the quick will recede and be easier to avoid. Here, you try it."

To my knowledge, they don't teach you how to trim a dog's toenails in acting school. It's obvious my mother knows what she's doing.

Lauren carefully follows Mom's example. Then Mom takes a steel file from the drawer and shows her how to file the pup's nails smooth. "Great job, Lauren. Just don't put any polish on those nails!" Mom says with a wink when they're done.

Gran returns, and I set Shirley on the table for her examination. "Your puppy's in great shape," Gran pronounces. "And she's obviously got a superb temperament. Just give her good care, consistent training, and lots of love."

"Oh, I will," Lauren says as she snuggles Shirley into her arms, clearly thrilled and relieved. Shirley licks her cheek.

As we wash our hands in preparation for the next patient, I prepare to eat crow. "OK, I guess you do know a bit about animals," I murmur to Mom. "I had no idea." I'm impressed and oddly pleased, but I also can't help feeling a bit annoyed. It's as if there's a whole side of Mom, an animal side, that she's held back from me all these years.

"Why do you think I was so good at playing a nurse on the soap opera?" she says lightly, handing me a towel. "My mother is a doctor!"

Gran chuckles. She's more relaxed around Mom than I expected. Although she's never criticized Mom to me, I sense that she didn't exactly approve of Mom leaving me to go off to Lala-land. All their phone calls over the past year started out friendly, but then Gran would begin to look serious and turn away, and finally she'd carry the phone into another room. Before I moved in with Gran, I don't think she and Mom ever talked on the phone, at least not that I saw. I've never quite known what came between them, but the way Gran's always so tight-lipped about Mom's career, I get the feeling that Gran didn't want her daughter to become an actress.

Gran steps out to fetch her next client and returns with a tall woman carrying an Abyssinian cat. As Mom steadies the slender brownish gold cat on the table and scratches its neck soothingly, Gran peers into its large ears with a light scope.

"Looks like Abby has ear mites," Gran says to the woman. "Zoe, would you please get the ear mite medication from the cabinet?"

As Gran puts drops in the cat's ear, the conversation turns to parrots. "My daughter lives on Telegraph Hill, in San Francisco," the woman is saying. "She told me there's an entire population of parrots living there wild. That surprised me alright—I thought parrots could only live wild in the tropics."

Gran hands the ear ointment back to me. "Apparently they're very adaptable," she replies.

Adaptable—that's the perfect word for Mom. Look how well she's adapted to life in California. And now she walks into this clinic, where she hasn't set foot in twenty years, and makes herself right at home.

I guess maybe the word could apply to me, too. When I first arrived at Gran's, I thought I'd never get used to it, but I did.

After a few more patients, the waiting room is finally empty, and Mom and I collapse on the waiting room couch for a breather. It occurs to me that Mom might be thirsty after her long trip. "Lemonade?" I offer.

"Oh, Zoe, that would be wonderful."

I pop next door to the kitchen and return a moment later with two glasses.

"Thank you, darling—this is just what I needed." She takes a drink and then gives a contented sigh. "My, but that puppy was sweet. You know, I'd forgotten how nice it feels to work with animals."

My mother never ceases to amaze me. "Mom, I always thought you didn't like animals."

She raises her eyebrows at me, just the way Gran does. "Whatever made you think that?"

"Well, we could never have a pet in New York, even though I wanted one and they were allowed in our building."

Mom nods and swirls the ice in her glass. Finally she says quietly, "Well, I was always so busy, and Ethel had enough to do without cleaning up after a pet, and—" She pauses, takes another drink, and then looks at me. "Animals die, Zoe. Sooner or later, they die. I couldn't—I didn't want you to feel that pain, that loss." She smiles at me, but the smile seems sad.

* * * * * * *

That afternoon Mom takes me and Maggie and David to the Ambler Bowl-a-Rama.

The guy at the desk recognizes Mom from her soap and makes a big fuss. Turns out they went to high school together, and he's thrilled when she lets him take a snapshot of the two of them standing in front of the lanes. "I'm gonna blow it up, frame it, and display it on the wall!" he declares. "Then the next time you come, you can sign it for me!"

Mom actually blushes, but she looks flattered by the attention.

"I bet they never had a TV star in here before," Maggie says as we head for our lane.

"Hey, I wasn't exactly a star," Mom says. "And besides, I'm off duty tonight. I'm just plain old Rose Hopkins, hometown girl."

When we get our rental shoes, it turns out Mom and I now wear the same size. Cool—that means I can start borrowing her shoes. She has a great collection.

"I didn't know you liked to bowl," I say as we lace up our bowling shoes.

"There are a lot of things you don't know about me," she says with a playful smile.

I realize it's true. I also sense that something about our relationship has changed. It's not just that I'm almost as tall as she is and wear the same size shoes. It's as if we've reached a new level in the way we relate to each other. We're still mother and daughter, of course, but now it's almost like we're friends, too—or could be if we weren't so far apart all the time. Suddenly I long to learn all those things about her that I don't know, such as the fact that she can clip a dog's toenails and calm a nervous cat. And I realize I want her to get to know me, too.

David comes over with a huge plate of nachos and a cardboard tray of sodas from the snack bar. "It's on the house!" he announces, impressed.

"Ah, one of the perks of fame!" Mom says dramatically, pulling off a big wad of chips and gooey cheese from the plate. Nachos are one of my secret weaknesses. Who knew they were Mom's, too?

As Maggie writes our names on the score sheet, Mom snares a swirly blue bowling ball. "Prepare to get creamed," she announces. She stares down the lane, takes a few steps, and rolls the ball.

Crash! A strike on her first roll.

"Whoa!" Maggie exclaims. I'm so unathletic that Maggie probably never guessed my mother might have athletic skills. A competitive gleam shines in my cousin's eyes. "How'd you do that, Aunt Rose?"

Mom grins. "I used to bowl in a league when I lived here. If you think Ambler's small now, you should have seen it when I was a kid. There was *nothing* else to do in the winter besides bowl!"

We play several games, switching partners each time, because everybody wants to be on Mom's team. When Maggie pairs up with Mom against David and me, they hammer us so badly that David and I simply devote our turns to inventing crazy new styles of rolling the ball while Maggie and Mom laugh hysterically at us. It makes me feel good to see that the other kids like my mother.

That evening after dinner, Gran turns to me. "Zoe, why don't you and Rose take Sneakers for a walk? Maggie and I will clean up."

I glance out the window. There are dark clouds in the distance. "It looks like it might rain."

"So take an umbrella. Sneakers needs the exercise. And I'm sure Rose would enjoy seeing the old neighborhood." She gives me a pointed, don't-argue-about-it look.

OK, I get it—this is where Mom and I are supposed to have some time alone together.

I go to get the leash.

* * * * * * *

"Sneakers! Cool it!" The walk is more like a drag—as in Sneakers dragging me down the street, acting up, and ignoring my commands.

I want Mom to see how special he is and love him as much as I do. He would pick this moment to misbehave.

But Mom doesn't seem to notice. She's talking a mile a minute about the new house, how I've grown, her job, my hair, the new school, her agent. Mom's always been the chatty type—she can charm anybody with her sparkling conversation—but she's setting a new world record for words per minute.

It couldn't be that she's nervous now that we're alone together, could it?

I, on the other hand, haven't said a word for ten minutes. Does she notice? After all, back in Manhattan she used to take me everywhere, so I met actors, producers, restaurant chefs, all kinds of VIPS, and I've learned how to talk to just about anybody. Yet now I feel tongue-tied around my own mother.

"...And it's wonderful being so near the ocean," Mom is telling me. She sighs happily. "I know it's taken a long time, but everything has finally fallen into place the way I'd hoped. I can't wait for you to see the house. Maybe next weekend we can go shopping and pick out furniture for your room—"

"You're coming back here next weekend?" Wow—this *is* a surprise.

"No...I meant go shopping in Los Angeles," Mom says slowly.

I stop and frown, puzzled. "I'm going out there for a visit?"

Mom bites her lip. "I didn't explain myself

very well, did I. What I mean to say is, I want you to fly back to California with me now, for good. I've waited so long for this moment. Now that we've got a house to move into, I just can't wait another minute to start our new life together." She beams at me and takes my hand.

I feel like a deer caught in a car's headlights. I thought I was surprised when she showed up this morning, but now I'm—stunned.

Mom keeps beaming at me. I want to share her joy and excitement, but somehow I can't. Still, I have to say something. "*Now?* Gosh, Mom, I—um—I guess I didn't realize it would be so—soon. I mean, it's a big move, and school's not out yet, and…" Suddenly, all the reasons *not* to go start pounding through my head: Maggie doesn't want me to leave. I don't want to leave *her*—or Gran. Besides, I still have to catch E.T. and find him a home, and get the parrot-protection program going, and…

The leash jerks, and Sneakers yanks me off the path to chase a chipmunk. It's his favorite game. He's never actually caught one; I think he just loves the chase. The chipmunk zips up a tree, and Sneaker stands upright against the trunk, pawing the tree and barking, as though he wanted to follow the chipmunk right up into the branches.

I wonder if Los Angeles has chipmunks. Otherwise, what will Sneakers chase—cars?

I finally convince him to give it up, and we rejoin Mom on the sidewalk. "Is there a quarantine for new dogs there?" I ask.

My mother looks puzzled. "Where?"

"In California."

"I—I'm not sure what you mean, Zoe." Mom's voice sounds oddly strained.

"What I mean is, will Sneakers have to spend some time in quarantine before he can move in with us? Some places do that, you know."

A cloud moves across the sun, and Mom shivers. "Zoe, it's not as if California's a different country. Though I do have to say, it's quite a bit warmer than here," she says lightly. "Listen, honey—"

Uh-oh. That's how she always starts bad news. I cut her off. "Sneakers *will* be coming too, won't he?"

"Now, Zoe—"

"Why not?" I demand, before she even gets the word *no* out.

There's a long pause.

"I just don't think it would be a good idea right now," she says quietly.

I look at Sneakers prancing ahead of us, his ears flopping. A lump swells in my throat. "Why?"

"Well, things will be rather unsettled for a while. Moving, getting you into a new school ...and my schedule will be very demanding." She pauses again, searching for words, then says firmly, "Dogs need consistency. They need a routine. They need someone who's going to be there for them and take care of them every day."

Sounds like she's quoting Gran.

I watch Sneakers rushing from side to side, as if every new smell is something to chase. "Sneakers needs *me*," I say hotly. "He was a homeless, half-dead, starving stray, and I took him in and brought him back to life. *I'm* his routine. I'm his home—his family."

"Zoe, dear, I think he would miss Gran and Maggie and the other animals—"

Oh, and I *won't*?

"—and that nice big backyard—"

"You said our house has a nice backyard!"

"It does, honey, but it's small, and it's not fenced. Wilshire Boulevard is a very busy street—

the cars go so fast, and..." Her voice seems to quiver, then trails off.

"Those are just lame excuses!" I retort. "You're thinking only about what's convenient for you. As usually, you're not even considering how I feel!"

"Zoe!" Mom exclaims, trying to put on a scolding-mom voice. But it's bad casting. She's uneasy in the role. She's never been that kind of mom.

"You just don't get it!" I practically shout at her. "I love Sneakers! I don't know what I would have done without him this past year. Sometimes I was so homesick. Sneakers was always there for me—when *you* weren't!"

Mom looks as though I've slapped her. "How can you say that?" she whispers.

"Easily! *You're* the one who hasn't been around for almost a year. I have my own life here now, Mom, with Gran and Maggie—and Sneakers. You can't just waltz in whenever it's convenient for you and start changing my life around!"

Mom freezes, and I can tell I've hurt her. But I don't care. Now maybe she understands how badly she hurt *me* when she went away.

"That's enough, Zoe," she says quietly. "Like it

or not, I'm your mother, and it's my job to make decisions for us."

"Your *job*?!" I scowl and turn away from her, so angry I'm afraid of what I might say next. Is it just my imagination, or is the sky getting darker by the second?

She hesitates, then rests her hands lightly on my shoulders. "Sweetie, I know I've been busy. I know I should have called you more often. But with the three-hour time difference, by the time I'd finally get home in the evening, it was usually much too late to call." Her voice is so wistful, it almost makes me feel guilty for being mean to her. "Oh Zoe, I've worked so hard for this—this job, and this house—but it means nothing to me if you're not there to share it with me. I want you to come home."

I've waited so long to hear those words, yet now, instead of making me happy, they're just making me upset and confused. I grip Sneakers's leash, blinking hard and willing myself not to cry.

She doesn't even know me anymore. She'll never understand how important Sneakers and everybody at Dr. Mac's Place are to me. And besides, who knows how long her job will last?

If her series is cancelled, then where will we go?

"I'm not leaving Sneakers," I announce. "And I'm not leaving the clinic, either."

"Zoe, be reasonable—"

"No, Mom! Go have your wonderful career in Hollywood if you want. But I'm not going anywhere."

Sneakers is delighted when I bolt for home. It looks like it's about to storm, anyway.

Mom doesn't run after me. And I don't look back.

Chapter Seven

. . . .

I wake up early, before my alarm goes off. In my dream, thousands of people were squawking at me, telling me where to go and what to do.

I blink my eyes and get a wet tongue in the face. "Morning, Sneak."

He gives me that little whine, the one that tells me *it's time to go.* The rapid wag of the tail means now—*as in five minutes ago.*

I roll out of bed, slide my feet into the leopard-print slippers Mom gave me for Christmas, and follow Sneakers downstairs. Out the backdoor window, I see that Mom and Gran are already awake and outside on the deck. Mom, up for sunrise? And why isn't Gran tending to her patients? I pad through the kitchen and peek out. They're sitting in the newly scoured deck chairs, sipping steaming mugs of coffee.

I open the door a crack, and Sneakers slips out and bounds onto the deck. He races to the tree, does his thing, then makes a sharp U-turn to run toward Mom, his tail wagging with interest in this still-new person.

"Sneakers!" I call him back. We are still mad at her. In fact, we aren't even talking to her.

Sneakers looks over at Mr. Cowan's yard and barks. He's answered by scolding squawks and shrieks. The parrots are back! I guess that explains the squawking in my dream—and why Mom and Gran are outside at dawn.

I open the door wider and peek out. The parrots have taken over Mr. Cowan's yard, clustered at the feeders and perched on his deck railing eating oranges. I send them some telepathy: *Hey, guess who cut up those oranges for you! Me, Zoe. I'm your friend!*

Padding across the yard in my slippers, I lean over the fence and scan the birds, searching for E.T. I want him to get some of the oranges.

The birds ignore me. They're too busy eating.

Wait a minute—there's a little green one with a blue head, right on Mr. Cowan's deck railing. "Phone home," I say softly, hoping that I don't scare them away—and that the blue-headed one will answer.

The other birds keep eating and don't react, but the one parrot swivels his little blue head toward me and blinks. It's got to be E.T.!

"Phone home," I repeat, crossing my fingers.

"Phone home!" the parrot squawks back. "Pretty girl! Time to fly!"

Yes! It's him. Thrilled, I turn to see if Gran and Mom noticed. But they've gone inside already. Oh well. I'd better go inside too and get ready for school.

• • • • • • •

At the breakfast table, Mom and Gran inform me that I am not going to school today.

I put down my toast. "How can you just decide these things without asking me?" I demand.

Gran's eyebrow shoots up and she gives me that warning look. She really dislikes mouthiness. "Sorry," I mumble. I'm not mad at her.

"We have lots to do," Mom explains. "Gran

will call your school and have your records sent out to the Beverly Hills School District, and you and I can start packing."

Very pleasantly and calmly, I explain back to her, "Even if I was leaving—which I'm not—I'd want to go to school to say good-bye to all my friends. Which I'm not going to do, because I am *not* leaving."

"Oh, Zoe, you can't be serious," Mom says, pouring herself more coffee.

It's as if she doesn't believe me. I feel my anger flare up again. "I've never been more serious in my life," I tell her, slowly and emphatically.

She looks a little taken aback, but just says, "There's no need to be so dramatic."

Even Gran has to laugh at *that* comment coming from an actress. Then she says, "I think you should stay home too, Zoe. We need a chance to talk and make plans. How about it?" She's obviously trying to smooth the conversation over before it blows up into a fight.

Late as usual, Maggie comes flying down the stairs just in time to hear this. "Can I stay home too?" she asks.

"No," Gran replies.

"No fair! Why not?"

"Do the words *math makeup test* ring a bell?" Gran says firmly.

Maggie glowers at me. "Lucky dog."

"Maggie, I actually want to go to school today." I can't wait to tell everyone about the parrots, and see if Brenna has any pictures, and discuss my parrot Web site idea with Sunita, and—

"Here." Maggie jams her baseball cap on my head. "Stuff your hair up, and you can go as me. Maybe you can ace my math test."

"No way." I toss the hat back at her like a Frisbee. She plunks it back on her head, slings her backpack over her shoulder, and grabs a piece of toast. She folds it like a taco to hold some scrambled eggs and begins stuffing it in her mouth as she heads for the door.

"Do you see what she's doing?" I ask Gran indignantly.

Gran sighs. "At least it's real food for a change."

"Have fun playing hooky," Maggie calls with her mouth full.

"Have fun taking your math test," I shout back as the front door slams.

"They're so cute," Mom says to Gran. "They remind me of the way Joanne and I used to fight, back when the MacKenzie sisters ruled the neighborhood." She smiles, but her eyes are sad.

Suddenly I feel a tiny bit sorry for being so mean to my mom. Joanne was Maggie's mother—and Mom's sister. I've never really thought about what it must have been like for Mom to lose a sister. She doesn't talk about it.

Maggie's the nearest thing I've ever had to a sister. I look out the front window at her standing at the bus stop, gabbing with David. I think about her stubborn, upturned nose covered with freckles, and about how we can squabble all the time and still stay close, just the way siblings do.

It would feel horrible to lose her.

Mom invites me to stay at the table and have a cup of tea with her, but I have nothing to say that I haven't already said. "Um, gotta take a shower," I mutter as I leave the kitchen. She doesn't comment on the fact that I was already dressed for school.

For a while I just stand in the shower thinking, letting the hot water pour down on me. Then I wash my hair, even though it's not really dirty. I get out and blow-dry it, even though I usually just let it air dry. After that I try on three different outfits before choosing one to wear.

Anything to delay going down to face my mother.

When I finally do get downstairs, Mom's on the phone. She whispers at me, "It's my agent. I'll be off in just a minute, honey."

Who is she kidding? This is not going to be a five-minute call.

Sitting at the kitchen counter, I scan through the classified ads for "Pets, Lost & Found," hoping nobody's looking for a lost parrot. I don't want E.T. to be lost, I want him to be abandoned. So I can adopt him. I cross my fingers as I read.

"Lost parrot." I bite my nail and read on. An Amazon. Good—that's much bigger than E.T. I read on down the column. Everything else is a cat or a dog.

"No lost blue-crowned conures," I inform Gran, who's at the sink washing the breakfast pans. "Looks like E.T. will need a new home after all."

Gran shakes her head. "You may not be able to catch him, Zoe."

What Gran doesn't understand is that E.T. likes me. I'm sure I can find a way to catch him.

"Here, wipe the bacon grease off the stove, please." Gran tosses me a soapy sponge.

I wipe down the stovetop and counter, and then hand the sponge back to Gran. Mom's still on the phone. I can sort of hear her muffled conversation through the closed door. I wonder what Gran thinks about this whole L.A. business?

I take a deep breath. "Gran, do you think I should go with my mom to Los Angeles?" I'm not sure what I want her answer to be.

She doesn't answer right away, which tells me she's not sure, either. Somehow it reassures me to know I'm not the only one feeling uncertain. Finally she says, "What I think about it isn't as important as what you think. How do *you* feel about moving?"

"Not good," I state. "It's not that I don't want to be with Mom. And a new place could be kind of interesting, I guess. But I don't want to leave you and Maggie and Dr. Mac's Place. And I refuse to leave Sneakers."

"It's never easy to leave people you love." Gran looks at me sympathetically. "On the other hand, living three thousand miles from your mother can't be easy for you, either."

"But Gran, do you really think living in

L.A. will be better for me than living here in Ambler?"

"It's not a question of which city is better to live in, Zoe. The question is, where will you be happier?"

"How should I know?" I snort. Do I look like a clairvoyant? Biting my lip, I remind myself that I'm not mad at Gran. "All I know is, Mom wants me to leave behind everything I love here. And she even wants to pull me out of school and force me to go to a big new school with barely six more weeks left in the school year. I don't want to do that!"

"Fine," Gran says. "Then that's what you need to tell her."

Gran always makes everything sound so simple, but it's never simple when I actually try to do it. "Can't *you* tell her?" I mumble.

A long, silent pause. Gran wrings out her dishcloth and sets it on the counter. Finally she turns and looks straight at me. For the first time since I've known her, her bright, clear blue eyes look clouded.

"Zoe, if I try to tell Rose what she should or shouldn't do, it won't help your case, believe me. I made that mistake long ago, and I learned my lesson. This is something only you can do. You need to talk with her and tell her exactly how you feel. Just remember, she loves you very much and truly does want the best for you."

"Could have fooled me." Sullenly I scuff my toe on the linoleum.

"Sometimes people do make bad decisions, Zoe, even though they may be trying to do the right thing. And sometimes"—Gran reaches for my hand—"what seems like a bad decision is actually a good one. Think about it: A year ago you wanted to go with Rose to California instead of moving in with me—perfectly understandable. You couldn't see why your mother would leave you with a grandmother who was a complete stranger to you. But looking back, don't you think your mother made the right decision when she sent you here?"

As usual, Gran's logic is undeniable. I give a tiny nod.

Gran ruffles my hair, then folds me into a hug. "Honey, your mother and I don't always see eye-to-eye. But there's one thing we agree on: we both want you to be happy. So you need to search your heart, figure out what you truly want, and then speak up." Gran lifts my chin. Her eyes are clear again, such a light, piercing blue. She smiles at me. "That's my prescription."

"OK, Dr. Mac, I'll try to follow it." *Try* being the operative word. Based on past experience, my hopes for success are not high.

The other line rings, and Gran picks up the kitchen phone. "This is Dr. MacKenzie."

Immediately her face takes on a serious expression. Must be a patient with an emergency. I start to leave the room, but she signals for me to wait. After a few minutes she thanks the caller and hangs up.

"That was the sheriff," she tells me. "He called to say they found an abandoned trailer in a ditch—with dead parrots inside it."

"How awful! What happened?"

"The police think the parrots were smuggled up from Mexico, and the driver was heading to New York to sell them—until he ran off the road. He was probably driving nonstop and hadn't slept for days. The trailer has been lying in the ditch for at least a week, but it's on a back road and nobody saw it until a farmer reported it."

As the information sinks in, I look up at Gran in horror. "Smuggled! Are you kidding?"

"I wish I were, Zoe. I hate to say it, but parrot

smuggling is big business. Since nearly all wild parrots are endangered, most countries have very strict rules about exporting and importing exotic birds. As a result, a large black market has developed in smuggled birds."

"But Gran, there are parrot breeders right here in the U.S.! Why would anyone want to smuggle in birds illegally?"

"Money—what else. A smuggler can buy a wild bird from a poacher in Mexico for maybe ten dollars, and then sell it here for fifty times that amount. So it's a highly profitable trade."

I shake my head, trying to make sense of this. "But if the parrots are so valuable, why would the trucker just abandon them?"

Gran shrugs. "He may not have had a choice. If the trailer came open in the crash, the birds may have just flown away on their own. Or maybe he knew he was going to go on the lam, so he took pity on the birds and let them loose."

"A smuggler, taking pity on the birds?" I say skeptically.

"The truck driver was probably not the smuggler," Gran explains. "Most likely he was just hired by the smuggling operation. If he had a wreck, he'd be in serious trouble—not only with the police, once they found what he was hauling, but also with whoever hired him."

"And the dead birds that the police found in the trailer—they died in the crash?"

"Could be," Gran says. "Or they might have been dead already, even before the accident. From what I know, a lot of birds die in smuggling operations, just from poor care and rough handling."

"But that's—that's beyond cruel! How can anyone just let animals suffer and die like that?"

Gran looks sadly at me. "Exotic animal smugglers are hardened criminals, Zoe. They see the parrots as a money-making commodity, like corn or coffee beans, not as living creatures. It's a terrible thing. And it's why so many countries now regulate trade in exotic birds. But unfortunately, there are always people willing to break the law if there's enough money at stake."

That's one piece of the puzzle that still doesn't quite fit. Obviously this whole underground bird trade is driven by dollars, but where does all that money come from? The answer slowly dawns on me: *the customer, the person at the end of the line who buys the parrot.* "Gran, who would buy an illegal bird?"

"Many people don't know the birds are smuggled when they buy them," Gran points out. "That's why parrot organizations and veterinarians urge people to buy a parrot only from a reputable pet store or breeder. But some people are so eager to have an exotic bird that they don't do their research. Or if the price is right, they're willing to look the other way."

Well, I guess now we know where our parrot flock came from. These really *are* wild birds, straight from the jungle. At least they'll have good survival instincts, even if this region is a totally strange environment to them.

"Can they track down the driver?" I ask Gran. "Maybe the police could convince him to turn in the smugglers in exchange for a light sentence."

"Well, they're trying to track him down," she says, "but the truck was a rental, so they may never find him."

Since Mom's still on the phone, I ask Gran, "Can I use the computer? I want to see what's on the Internet about parrot smuggling."

Gran checks her watch. "Mind if I look over your shoulder?"

Together we head into Gran's office. I key in *parrot smuggling*, and a long list of sites pops up. I click on one, and Gran and I read silently together.

As I read, I grow sadder—and angrier—by the minute. According to the Web site, more than 25,000 wild parrots are smuggled across the Texas border into the United States each year. The birds are sold in the U.S. for hundreds or even thousands of dollars at pet stores, flea markets, and exotic pet shows. Around 40 million dollars' worth of parrots are believed to be smuggled through Texas *each year*!

Gran lets out a low whistle. "You can see why some crooks think it's worth the risk."

"And look at this," I say, scrolling down. "It says that thousands and thousands of birds die from suffocation, starvation, or rough treatment while they're being smuggled in." I turn to Gran. "I just can't stand the thought of all those poor birds suffering. There must be *something* we can do about this!"

Gran blinks, then gives me a sad, almost wistful smile.

"What?" I say, puzzled.

"Oh, you suddenly reminded me of another girl I used to know."

"Somebody who used to work with you at the clinic?"

"Well, yes, actually." Gran gets a misty expression. "Your mother."

"I remind you of *Mom*?"

But before I can ask her about that, Mom herself charges into the office with a pad and pen in her hand, the cordless phone clutched between her ear and shoulder. "Ma, what's your fax number?"

Gran gestures at the fax machine sitting in a corner, buried under folders and books. "Sorry, Rose, it's broken. Hasn't worked in months."

"Ma, how can you run a business without a fax?" Mom shakes her head in exasperation. "There must be a copy shop around here where you can fax it to," she tells the caller. "I'll get a number and call you right back." She clicks off the phone and starts to leave, then turns to me. "Zoe, I'm going to run into Ambler. The producer needs to fax me some script changes for next week's taping." Then she adds hesitantly, "Want to come? We could stop for ice cream."

Gran looks at me, and I squirm. I know I should go with Mom. Here's my chance to tell her how I really feel, like Gran said. The only problem is, I don't know how I really feel. So how can I tell Mom what I want, if I'm not even sure myself?

"I—I'm kind of busy right now, Mom. I'm, uh, doing some research on parrots. It's really important. But thanks anyway. Maybe we can, um, discuss our plans when you get back," I finish lamely.

"OK, sounds good." She throws me one of her chipper smiles and heads out the door.

Gran stands up and stretches. "Well, Zoe, patients start arriving in about ten minutes, so I'll be off too." I can tell she's disappointed in me for not joining Mom.

Well, I can live with that. I mean, after everything I've just learned about smuggled parrots, their well-being somehow seems more important right now than my own problems. After all, it's a life-and-death matter for the parrots.

Turning to the computer, I go back to the search engine and key in *feral parrots*. "Feral" means an animal that's escaped and is living wild. I learned that when Maggie, Sunita, David, Brenna, and I discovered a huge pack of feral cats living in an abandoned boxcar last fall.

The first site I visit tells all about the Monk parakeets in Chicago. The people who are studying them make a big point of saying there's no evidence of the birds causing crop damage in the U.S. That's good to know. I'll have to tell Mr. Cowan.

Then I read about the parrots in San Francisco. Apparently there's not one but *two* flocks there. I hop from site to site with growing excitement. There are parrot flocks in Texas, in Rhode Island, in Florida, and even—my heart starts pounding—in Southern California! In fact, I stumble across a major Web site, the California Parrot Project, devoted to "researching parrots in the wilds of California's suburban jungles." Who knew?!

The people working on the California Parrot Project seem to be mostly scientists and professional researchers. For years they've been studying the feral parrot flocks, which they call "naturalized," so they know a lot about parrots living wild in city neighborhoods. My mind starts spinning with ideas. If I were living in Southern California, I could volunteer with this organization and help the wild parrots out there. And I could share what I learn with Maggie and Gran and everyone at Dr.

Mac's Place, so they could help the parrots here in Ambler…

I shut down the computer and race downstairs, looking for Gran. Oops, she's busy with patients. Drat, I can't even tell Maggie or my friends—they're all at school. I'm bursting to talk to someone about all my parrot ideas! I even want to tell Mom, but she's not back yet. How about Mr. Cowan? I have to tell him about the sheriff's call anyway, and I know he'll be interested to hear what I've learned about parrots living wild in the U.S. Plus, we need to put out more fruit. I wonder if parrots like grapes? I grab some from the fridge and head out the back door.

* * * * * * *

"Pretty girl!"

I close the back door behind me quickly, before Socrates escapes, and step onto the deck. "E.T.!" I whisper excitedly. "Where've you been?"

He perches on the fence between our yard and Mr. Cowan's and cocks his head at me. I love his bright blue head and the way his beak is orange on the upper part and black on the lower. He's so cute! And smart, too—I can tell by the way he watches me. It's as if we are playing a game and he's daring me to try and catch him.

Dr. Timmons's words came back to me: *The odds of a hand-fed bird surviving for very long in the wild are slim...*

Now's your chance, Zoe, I tell myself.

I approach E.T. slowly, talking quietly. "Hello, E.T. Good boy. I won't hurt you..." I hold out my arm and show him the grapes in my hand. If he's used to people, maybe he'll fly to me, just as he used to fly to his owner. "Come on," I whisper. "Please?"

But he doesn't come to me. Instead, he gives me a Bronx cheer—"Brwaak!"—then flutters his wings and swoops into Mr. Cowan's yard.

I hesitate a second, then unlatch the gate and follow him. As quietly as possible, I sneak across Mr. Cowan's yard. There's no sign of Mr. Cowan, but I'm afraid to call him or go and get him— that might scare E.T. away.

E.T. starts eating some nuts Mr. Cowan spread out on the railing of his deck. *Good, just stay right there, E.T., where I can reach you.* I realize I don't have a towel to wrap around him, the way Gran did the other day with Pickles. Maybe my sweat-shirt will do. I ease it off over my head, then slowly, slowly move forward, one step at a time, barely daring to breathe. I'm so close…

How exactly did Gran capture Pickles? Now that I'm just a few feet from E.T., I realize catching him will not be as easy as Gran made it look. Heart pounding, I exhale slowly. E.T. cocks his head at me.

I freeze.

He ruffles his feathers, watching me warily.

The moment is now—I've got to do something before he flies off. I lunge toward him, throwing my sweatshirt over him like a net.

Startled, E.T. struggles beneath the thick fabric, squawking in alarm. I try to pick up the shirt with the bird in it, but he struggles so much, it frightens me. He's much bigger and stronger than I thought—and I realize with a sinking feeling that it's not so easy to just grab a bird when you've never even held one before. I keep thinking of Gran's warning: *If you squeeze his chest too tightly you can suffocate him.* What if I grab him the wrong way?

Now E.T. is so frightened, he's screaming and shrieking and oh, my gosh, this is not turning out the way I wanted! But I've got to do something. I snatch him up, and his head pokes out. Just as I'm remembering what Dr. Timmons said about having powerful beaks, E.T. clamps his beak on my wrist. It hurts! Without meaning to, I gasp and drop the sweatshirt onto the deck, with E.T. still in it.

With ear-splitting shrieks, E.T. fights his way out from under the shirt and manages to crawl free. He beats his wings to escape, looking disoriented. He takes flight but suddenly veers sideways, smashes into the sliding glass door, and falls to the ground.

Chapter Eight

· · · · · · · · · · · ·

The small bird lies on Mr. Cowan's deck, not moving. I'm afraid to touch him, afraid I'll hurt him more.

What have I done?!

I run back to our yard, shouting urgently, "Gran—help!" Can she hear me from the clinic? "Help!"

Suddenly Mom bolts onto our deck. "Zoe! Are you all right?"

I shake my head, tears streaming down my cheeks. "Mom, it's E.T. He's hurt."

"Where?"

"Next door." I dash back across the lawn and through the gate, with Mom right behind me. When we get to Mr. Cowan's deck, I point at the green bird, still lying motionless. "I tried to catch him and he flew into the window. Oh Mom, what if he's—" I hiccup and start to sob.

Mom kneels down beside E.T. My sweatshirt's still lying near the railing, and I hand it to her. With a quick, smooth motion—just like Gran— she picks him up in the sweatshirt. I follow her as she walks swiftly back across the yard to the clinic.

Gran looks up as we barge into the exam room. "What's going on?" she asks. Fortunately she's between patients, but she looks a bit annoyed at the sudden intrusion.

"It's all my fault, Gran!" I blurt out. "I—I just wanted to help him…"

Silently Mom hands her the sweatshirt with the limp bird.

Gran lays E.T. out on the exam table. His eyes are closed. His wing looks crooked. And he's got blood on his chest.

"OK, Zoe, tell me what happened," Gran orders as she pulls out her stethoscope.

I tell her.

"Mmm," Gran says, a slight frown on her face as she examines the injured bird.

"I'm so sorry, Gran. All I could think about was rescuing him and making sure he has a good home," I say, blinking back tears. "I see now it was a bad idea." I wish desperately that I could turn back the clock and make E.T. whole again, happily eating nuts on Mr. Cowan's deck. I think of what Gran said to me this morning: *Sometimes people do make bad decisions, Zoe, even though they may be trying to do the right thing.* Boy, was she ever on the money.

"Come on, E.T., wake up," Gran murmurs. She looks at me and Mom. "There's a heartbeat, so there's still hope. But with head trauma, if a bird's unconscious more than a few minutes, he usually won't make it."

Mom takes my hand, and I glance at her. Her eyes are wet, too.

"Please, E.T.," I whisper. "Don't die on me!"

Mom and Gran exchange a look. I can see they're thinking the worst.

No. I can't bear it if he dies. I'll be the one who killed him. Come on, E.T., I beg silently.

Please give me a chance to learn the right way to hold you.

A feather twitches.

I hold my breath. Is he awake? I lean forward, staring at the little white patch encircling his closed eye. *Come on, please!*

He twitches. I hold my breath. He twitches again—and then opens his eye and blinks at me.

"He's awake!" I whisper.

"And," Gran adds, with a big smile, "if he wakes up, he'll probably make it." She quickly gives E.T. a shot of cortisone, which, she explains, will help shrink any brain swelling from the head trauma.

"What about all that blood on his chest?" I ask.

"There does seem to be rather a lot, and it certainly looks ominous, but I don't see any wound on his chest," Gran says, gently turning the bird over. "His cere—that's the area above his beak—isn't bloody, so I don't think he's bleeding from the nostrils, which is good. But look, he's damaged the tip of his beak. That's where the blood's coming from. It must have happened when he hit the window. I'll just cauterize the end of it and it should be fine."

"Really?" I exhale with relief.

"It's not unusual," Gran explains. "Lots of blood, but no lasting damage. It can be life threatening if the bleeding isn't controlled, though."

Gran gently extends one wing and then the other. E.T. gives a weak squawk. "Yup, I know, you've got a broken wing. We'll set that for you in a little bit."

Gran puts E.T. into the oxygen cage, just as she did with Pickles. When he comes out, he seems a little stronger, so Gran takes an X-ray of his wing.

I roll the anesthesia machine into the X-ray room. On one end of the machine is a long, thin tube with a small plastic cone attached to the end. Before slipping the cone over the bird's head, Gran does something weird: she takes a rubber surgical glove and ties the fingers together, then snips a small cut in the hand of the glove.

Puzzled, I ask Gran what she's doing.

Gran smiles. "What would happen if I put this cone over E.T.'s head?"

I frown and study the cone. Then I see the

problem. The cone is sized for dogs and cats. If Gran were to put it over E.T.'s little head, "The gas would leak out," I reply.

Nodding, she stretches the open end of the glove—the part you put your hand in—over the cone. Then she carefully slips the small cut opening over E.T.'s beak and face, until his entire head is inside the glove.

I figure E.T. will freak out, but he seems perfectly calm. "Why isn't he afraid?" I ask.

"Most birds become completely quiet and docile in the dark," Gran says. "They just think it's time to sleep. And, of course, the gas takes effect right away."

Mom settles the limp bird on a cassette of X-ray film, chest up. Gran spreads his wings out and, to my surprise, tapes them down with masking tape. When she sees my surprised expression, she explains, "It sticks to everything but feathers."

E.T. keeps sleeping, breathing in the gas, and Gran lets me check his heartbeat with her stethoscope to make sure it's normal. Then she hustles us all out of the room, so we won't be exposed to the radiation, and quickly pushes the pedal to shoot the X-ray. Mom and I go back in to E.T., and I check his heart rate again—about 300 beats a minute, just what Gran said it should be.

A few minutes later, Gran returns from the darkroom. She holds up the X-ray, and it clearly shows the breakage in E.T.'s wing. Gran says it's in the "radius," which is basically the same bone we have in our forearms. Quickly Gran positions the wing and wraps it against the parrot's body with a cloth bandage so it can heal. She gives E.T. an injection for pain, and then Mom removes the glove from his head, stopping the gas. In about a minute, E.T. comes to.

I prepare a cage with water and food, and Gran places him inside. "He'll have a rough day or two," she says, "but soon he'll be almost as good as new. The wing should heal in three or four weeks."

Mom and I carry E.T.'s cage into a dark, quiet room where he can rest and recuperate in a peaceful environment.

We peek into his cage to say good night. "Do you think he's really going to be all right? " I ask Mom.

Mom puts her arm across my shoulders. "I think he'll be fine."

• • • • • • •

That night, Mom and I sit on my bed in our pj's, and Mom tells me all about how she and Joanne used to help Gran at Dr. Mac's Place, just as Maggie and I do now. It's funny how life sometimes comes full circle, often in the ways you least expect.

Sneakers leaps onto the bed with us, and I'm amazed when Mom scoops him into her arms. All my life, she's avoided having anything to do with animals, yet I saw how concerned she was about E.T. today, and now here she is snuggling with Sneakers! I can't stand it anymore. I have to ask her the burning question: "Mom, why don't you want Sneakers to come to Los Angeles?"

"Zoe, I told you—"

"I know you'll be busy, but I'm old enough to take care of Sneakers myself. I already do!"

"I know, honey, you've done a great job with Sneakers. But—" She falters, then continues. "If anything should happen to him—"

"That's your whole concern? You didn't want me to keep Sneakers because he's going to die someday?" I can't quite buy this explanation. Mom's a risk taker. Since when has a risk ever held her back from doing something she wanted?

Then Mom gets that sad look in her eyes again,

and suddenly I wish I could snatch my question back. "Never mind, you don't have to answer that. It's none of my business," I murmur.

"No, I should tell you. It's just…hard to talk about."

"Gran says I'm a good listener," I say encouragingly.

Mom smiles, then begins. "I had a dog once. I named her Lady. She was a stray that showed up in the neighborhood. We wound up adopting her—"

"Just like Sneakers!"

"Yes, I suppose so." Mom takes a deep breath, then continues. "I'd always begged for my own pet, and finally Ma and Pop agreed. I took her everywhere." She pats my bed. "She even slept with me, at the foot of this very bed. I loved that dog."

I swallow. Something bad is coming.

"Ma always nagged me about keeping her on a leash when we were out. But Lady didn't really like the leash, so when I took her on walks where Ma couldn't see us, I'd let her loose." Mom stares off in the distance. "Oh, Zoe, you should have seen her run. She could really move."

Mom doesn't say any more for a few moments. At last I whisper, "What happened to her?"

"One day I let her off the leash and she ran into the street..." Mom shrugs her shoulders and blinks back tears.

She doesn't have to tell me what happened.

"Ma and Pop told me not to blame myself, that it was an accident. But I knew it was my fault. I swore I'd never have another pet. Because I couldn't bear to feel that kind of sorrow again." Her voice almost a whisper, she adds, "And I never, ever wanted to hurt another animal."

I think about all the family members she's lost in her life since losing Lady: Her dad, who died when she was ten. Joanne, her sister. Not to mention my dad, who left her when I was a toddler.

"Sometimes it's just easier not to have something, even if it's something you might want," she says.

I can't help it—I have to ask: "Is that why it was so easy for you to leave me?"

"Zoe! Is that what you think? *No,* it wasn't easy—it was the hardest thing I've ever done. And it was only supposed to be for a little while. I never planned on it being this long." She takes my face in her hands. "Oh, sweetheart, I wish I could go back and redo this year. I know I made some promises I couldn't keep. You see, if I'd known we'd be apart for nearly a year, I never would have done it. The whole time, I wanted to believe that you'd be coming out soon, so I just acted as if it were true. But I was fooling myself, and it was horribly unfair to you." She takes a big breath. "I want you back home with me, Zoe. Seeing you here, it's really hit me how much you've grown up since we left New York. And I don't want to miss another minute."

"Oh, Mom."

We hold each other for a few minutes without saying a word. Then she asks softly, "What do you think, Zoe? Do you want to come home now?"

For a moment I hold my breath. I wish I could be in two places at once. Or somehow blend both places into one.

But I have to make a choice. And I've made up my mind. I know what I want to do.

Chapter Nine

• • • • • • • • • • •

"Hurry *up!*" Maggie hollers up the stairs on Wednesday morning.

"Don't you mean hurry *down*?" I yell back at my cousin from the second floor, just to annoy her.

Sunita runs up the stairs to my room, holding a stack of folded shirts. "These were on the dryer. Do they go in a suitcase?"

I groan. "Mom," I call over my shoulder, "how could you possibly wear eight shirts in three days?"

"Zoe, honey, do you know where my contacts are?" is her only reply.

"Check your purse," I say, shaking my head.

Really, I don't know how she got along without me this past year. When I get to California,
things are going to be different.

Because I've decided: I'm going to move to
L.A. with her. Only I'm not going right away.

Mom and I talked for a long time Monday
night. I finally summoned the nerve to ask her
what came between her and Gran. It's as I sus-
pected: Gran never wanted Mom to be a professional actress. In fact, they had colossal fights
about it, especially when Mom dropped out of
college to go to New York. Gran knew that show
business is a hard profession and very few actors
make it. She'd always hoped Mom would go to
vet school and eventually come to work in the
clinic with her. But after Lady died, Mom just
turned away from animals completely.

Talking about all these painful events of the
past, especially with Sneakers right there on
the bed with us, seemed to help Mom come
around to the idea that it might be OK to have a
pet again. I told her about how my friend Jane's
dog, Yum-Yum, died of cancer last fall, right
around the time Sneakers came into my life. Jane
was incredibly sad to lose Yum-Yum, but—as I

pointed out to Mom—that didn't mean Jane was sorry she'd ever had Yum-Yum for a pet. I think this helped Mom realize that I've seen animals die and that I'm old enough to have some perspective on it and be able to handle it when it happens.

So when school is out, in about six weeks, Sneakers and I will be moving out to California. Gran says she might even take a rare vacation and come with us to see Mom's new place. I want Maggie to come, too. Maybe she can even stay for part of the summer.

Since Mom won't be seeing me for another six weeks, she decided to stay here one more day with Gran and me. We had a great day yesterday. First, Mom and I slept in, because we were up talking half the night. I got to play hooky again, and since the clinic wasn't very busy, Gran left Dr. Gabe in charge and we all went out for lunch. ("In L.A. they call this 'doing lunch,'" Mom informed us.) In the afternoon, while Mom studied her new script, I visited Mr. Cowan and told him all about the sheriff's phone call and what happened to E.T. Mr. Cowan liked my ideas for encouraging people around Ambler to put out fruit and vegetables for the parrots, along with birdseed.

Today, as soon as we get back from taking Mom to the airport, I'm going to e-mail the California Parrot Project and ask about volunteer opportunities out there. Sunita has already told me she'd be glad to set up and run a Web site for our Ambler parrots, to keep track of the flock and educate the public about the birds. So when I move out to L.A., I'll be able to check on the Ambler parrots anytime, just by going to the Web site.

As I head downstairs, David pops his head into the hallway from the clinic door. "Uh, is this parrot supposed to be out of its cage?"

"E.T.!" I don't have to ask which of our feathered patients he's referring to. Pickles is a quiet, cooperative bird, but E.T. is an escape artist. That's probably how he got loose from his former owner. Dr. Gabe has nicknamed him Houdini. "I'll go get him," I tell David.

"Time to fly!" E.T. squawks as I gently return him to his cage. Yesterday Gran showed me how to hold a bird, and I practiced on Pickles.

"You got that right!" I laugh. "It's my mom you need to tell!"

E.T. looks like he's going to recover almost

as quickly as his namesake did in the movie. We've notified all the animal shelters, and we're going to run a "found" ad in the newspaper, just in case. If nobody claims him, Gran says maybe—just maybe—I can take him with me to California. I think she realizes I'm determined to become an expert on parrots, and by the time I leave, I'll know enough about parrot care to be able to give him a good home.

Meanwhile, we have a foster father lined up for Pickles: Mr. Cowan. That way Pickles can have more company during his quarantine, so he doesn't get too bored and lonely, and Gran can free up her quarantine room. Once Pickles is fully recovered and the quarantine period is over, Mr. Cowan will reintroduce him to the flock. That will be right around the time school's out, just before I move, so I'll get to see Pickles reunited with his flock. It should be interesting to watch.

"Leaving in eight minutes!" Gran says, tapping her foot and looking at the clock.

Mom dashes in, holding up her contact case in triumph. "Found them! Socrates was sitting on the case. I swear, it's as if he were deliberately trying to make me miss my plane!"

Knowing Socrates, that wouldn't surprise me. He understands more than people give him credit for.

"He's not the only one who wishes you could stay longer," I mumble.

"Oh, honey, I wish I didn't have to go back already." Mom starts to look teary eyed.

"Don't cry," I scold her. "You're filming tomorrow. The director will have a cow if you show up with puffy eyes." She laughs and gives me a hug.

"Break it up, you two," Gran says. "You can do your crying in the van—if we ever get in it."

"I don't know what there is to cry about," David says to me as he picks up Mom's suitcase. "You're moving out there in less than two months."

"Don't talk about that now," Sunita says, "or we'll all start bawling!"

I get a lump in my throat. Sunita's right. I know that moving home with Mom is the right decision, but it's going to be hard to leave Dr. Mac's Place.

At least this way I'll have some time to say good-bye.

Bird Words

By J.J. MACKENZIE, D.V.M.

Wild World News—People love to listen to parrots talk. But are these birds just clever copycats? Or do they have the intelligence to understand what they're saying?

Smart Alex. One of the most famous talking parrots is an African Grey named Alex. In 1977, Dr. Irene Pepperberg began working with Alex when he was one year old. Her training methods required Alex to do more than just mimic—he had to connect words to their meanings. For example, if Alex said "key," Dr. Pepperberg gave him a key, not a reward of food. When he performed well, he was rewarded with food, but only when he asked for the treat by name.

Today, after 20 years of work, Alex can identify and name more than 40 objects, such as paper, wood, key, banana, nut, rock, cup, and carrot. He can even distinguish color and shape. For example, in one experiment a tray holds a plastic key and a metal key. If

Dr. Pepperberg asks, "What toy?" Alex will answer, "Key." If she asks, "How many?" Alex will answer, "Two." Then she rewards him with an almond, his favorite treat.

Alex can do more than identify objects. If he asks for something—say, a banana—and the person hands him the wrong item, Alex will say "No" and repeat his request until he gets what he asked for.

Alex even teaches other birds how to talk to people. Dr. Pepperberg says that he rarely makes mistakes as a teacher and that the other birds actually learn faster from Alex than from human teachers!

Alex's language remains very simple. He cannot talk to his human friends the same way that people talk to each other. He cannot talk about how he feels or what he did yesterday. He cannot speak in sentences the way the parrot does in the fictional movie *Paulie*. Still, research like Dr. Pepperberg's does seem to tell us that parrots are far more intelligent than we ever imagined.

HOW TO TEACH A PARROT TO TALK
Not all parrots can become big talkers like Alex. But with hard work and lots of

patience, you can teach almost any parrot to say at least a few words. The chattiest parrots are African Greys, Amazons, and Macaws. Males usually talk more than females.

Here are some tips for teaching a parrot to talk:

Look who's talking. When choosing a new bird, ask yourself these questions:
• Does he seem interested in people?
• Does he look at you and listen when you speak?
• Does he already squawk and vocalize a lot?
A happy bird with an outgoing personality will be easier to teach.

Start early. The best time to begin is when the bird is six to twelve months old. A young, hand-raised bird is easier to teach than an older bird, although older birds can still be taught.

One on one. Birds are very social animals, and if you have another bird, the two birds might spend most of their time talking to each other in their own language. But if it's just you and one bird, your pet will be eager to socialize with you.

Be quiet. Turn off the TV and radio. Work in a quiet room without a lot of traffic or distractions.

Take it easy. Start with a simple one- or two-syllable word, such as *hello*. Say the word slowly, over and over, with a few seconds in between.

Short and sweet. A bird has a short attention span, so keep each training session brief—about 15 minutes. Two lessons a day are best. Early mornings and afternoons are good times to practice, because that's when birds are naturally most talkative.

Do it yourself. Some people use recordings of their voice to train their birds. But many bird enthusiasts don't recommend using this method. The bird may become so bored hearing the tape over and over that he begins to ignore it. Or he may learn to repeat the word, but he won't necessarily connect the activity of talking to people. Your goal is to teach your pet to talk and interact with you and other people.

Face to face. Stand right in front of your parrot. Make eye contact, and talk *to* your pet, not just at it. Speak clearly—your bird will learn to say the word exactly as you pronounce it!

Reward often. Have your bird's favorite treat handy, and reward him for even the smallest effort to say the new word. Don't worry if your bird mumbles or babbles in the beginning—that's a normal part of the learning-to-talk process. Once he learns to say his first word clearly, each new word will be easier to learn.

Have patience. It could take your bird as little as a week to learn his first word—or as long as two months or more! Each bird is an individual and will learn at his own pace.

Keep talking. Even when you're not having a lesson, chat with your bird when you're feeding him or cleaning his cage. Say hello when you come into the room. Praise him often and make him feel as if he's part of the daily life of the household. Your bird will be happier, and you'll reinforce the idea that talking is a positive aspect of your relationship.

Turn the page to read a sample of the next book
in the Vet Volunteers series...

Masks

Chapter One

. . . .

You'll make an awesome tiger, Sunita," Maggie tells me as we spread our art materials across her kitchen table. It's Thursday afternoon, a week before Halloween. We've decided we'd better start making costumes for the big Halloween party at the Ambler Town Center.

"Your dark eyes will look so cool through the mask," Maggie adds.

She's totally focusing on my costume now. Once Maggie sets her mind to a project, she locks in. Sometimes she reminds me of a bulldog— playful and fun, but once she sinks her teeth into something, it's awfully hard to shake her loose!

She studies me intently, working out my costume in her mind. "I've never seen a tiger with long black hair, though. Maybe we can make you an orange-striped hood to wear. Or a scarf out of tiger-striped fabric." She smiles. "Being a tiger is just perfect for you."

I'm surprised and pleased that Maggie sees me that way, but I'm not sure that being a tiger fits my personality. I think of tigers as fierce and strong. I'm more on the shy, timid side.

Being a tiger does fit with my number-one passion in life: cats. There are lots of other things I like—computers and computer games, ballet, reading (especially about animals), and collecting Ganesha statues. (Ganesha's a sweet Hindu god with a boy's body and an elephant's head.) But there's nothing I love more than cats—domestic cats, wild cats, large and small cats.

Another reason being a tiger fits me is that one home of the tiger is India, and that's where my ancestors came from. Both my mother and father are doctors who have lived in this country for many years, but we stay in touch with our Indian background.

There's a knock on the kitchen door, and Maggie opens it. David Hutchinson and Brenna

Lake come in. Brenna has a shopping bag stuffed with even more art supplies. She begins adding them to the pile of materials we've already loaded onto the table.

"Are you going to be a horse for Halloween?" I ask David. He's wild about horses.

He shakes his head. "A vampire. I vant to suck your blood!"

"He can't figure out how to make a horse mask," Brenna adds.

"I could too!" David objects. "I just think being a horse would be sort of geeky."

"Mucho geeky," Maggie agrees.

"What will you be?" I ask her.

"A vet, of course," Maggie replies.

"You don't need a mask for that," Brenna says.

"Yes, you do—a surgical mask. Gran has a ton of them in the supply cabinet," Maggie says.

"That's too easy. No fair," Brenna says. "I want to be something unusual—maybe a unicorn. Is that too babyish? I don't know. I still have to think about it."

Dr. Mac comes in and runs her hand through her short white hair as she surveys all our stuff—colored paper, yarn, glue, markers, beads and buttons, paints, pipe cleaners, and stickers. "Wow!" she says. "What's the big project?"

Dr. Mac is Dr. J.J. MacKenzie, veterinarian extraordinaire. She lives in a big brick house with Maggie. Although Dr. Mac is Maggie's grandmother, she's so full of energy that she doesn't seem like a regular grandmother to me.

Dr. Mac and Maggie live with lots of animals. Besides their cat, Socrates, and their dog, Sherlock Holmes, they have a house full of animal patients. That's because Dr. Mac runs Dr. Mac's Place Veterinary Clinic right here, attached to her own house. She treats any animals that come through the door—pets, strays, and even wild animals. People who bring in strays or wild animals pay her what they can or sometimes nothing at all.

I volunteer at Dr. Mac's Place, along with Maggie, David, and Brenna. I love working at the clinic. In fact, my dream is to be a vet someday.

"We're making masks for the Halloween party at Town Center," Maggie tells Dr. Mac. "Do you need us, Gran?"

Dr. Mac shakes her head. "So far it's been a slow morning. If something comes up, I'll holler," she says as she leaves the kitchen.

"Guess who I saw this morning?" Brenna asks as she redoes the elastic at the end of her long brown braid. She continues without waiting for an answer. "As I was coming here, I saw the woman who just moved into that big old converted barn down the road."

"Does she have any kids?" David asks.

Brenna shrugs her slim shoulders. "I didn't see any," she answers. "My mom heard that she's some kind of artist."

"That barn would be great for a studio," I say. "It's so big, and the last owners put in skylights."

"I saw the woman at the market," Maggie says, brushing her red hair out of her eyes. "She was wearing all black, and she has wild gray hair that makes her look like a witch!"

"Oh, my gosh!" Brenna cries. "Listen to this! When I saw her, she was pulling a big black kettle out of the back of her station wagon!"

"Oh, man, she's a witch for sure!" David says, his eyes lighting up.

Brenna wraps her arms around herself and shivers. "Whoa—a witch! And just in time for Halloween! Cool!"

"I can picture her with the black kettle," David

says. "Bubble, bubble, toil and trouble!" He mimics a cackling witch voice, pretending to stir an imaginary potion.

As David does his witch act, a black-and-white tuxedo cat strolls in. It's my cat, Mittens. I brought her with me this morning, because at my house repairmen are fixing our front steps, and all the hammering was scaring her. Mittens jumps up onto the table, and I scratch her between the ears. "Hi, honey," I murmur.

Before she was mine, Mittens was a stray. I first saw her one day when she came wandering around the clinic.

"Let's go check out the witch," David says. "I've never seen a real one."

"Oh, come on!" I say, laughing. "You don't really think she's a witch!"

"You never know," David says in a low, creepy voice, his eyes darting mysteriously from side to side. "At Halloween, anything is possible."

"David, you're so weird," I tease.

"I think there might really be such things as witches," Brenna says. "They can do good stuff, too."

"Yeah," Maggie agrees. "I mean, people have

believed in them for so long. Could people be totally wrong?"

"Sure they could be wrong!" I argue. "People used to think the earth was flat, and that the sun revolved around the earth, and all sorts of crazy things."

"I heard a story once," David begins in a spooky tone. "During the Salem witch trials, a woman was hanged for being a witch. But as they put the noose around her neck, she put this horrible curse on the people. She swore she would dance on their graves.

"Every year on the anniversary of her death, footprints appeared on the graves of anyone who had watched the witch get hanged. When people tried to wipe away the footprints, their hands were covered with blood."

"Ew!" Brenna cries with a shiver.

"Creepy," Maggie agrees.

I smile and roll my eyes. Spooky stuff like witches, ghosts, and ancient curses are fun at Halloween, but they're not for real. I'll take scientific explanations every time.

Mittens begins batting markers across the table. One of the markers rolls off and falls to the floor. As I bend to pick it up, Mittens starts chewing on a button. I pull it away from her. My cat has been known to eat strange things.

She pounces on my hand with her claws sheathed. "OK! OK! I get the message," I say to her. I pull a length of thick orange yarn out of its skein and cut it off. I dangle the yarn in front of Mittens. "Here you go, Mittens—catch this!"

I reach high and jiggle the yarn. Mittens rises on her back legs and swings her paws at it.

"Go on! Catch it!" I coax, pulling the yarn just out of her reach. "You can get it, Mittens." I lower the yarn just a bit so she can have the satisfaction of capturing it.

We laugh as Mittens pounces ferociously. She reminds me of a lioness, hunting out on the savanna. She snatches the whole piece of yarn out of my hand and then sits on it, protecting her prize.

"Good job!" we praise her, clapping. "Way to go!"

I stroke my cat's silky fur. I'd wanted a cat for so long before my mother finally gave in. At first, she had a million excuses—cats shed, cats tear up the furniture, and so on. When she finally let me have Mittens, it was the happiest day of my life.

I named my cat Mittens because she looks like she's wearing two little white mittens on her front paws.

I've never met a more affectionate cat. She's always nuzzling me and giving me scratchy little love-kiss licks. I return those with a kiss on her furry forehead.

David cuts a piece of white cardboard into the shape of a face. He cuts out the eyeholes, then a slit for the mouth. "Should I draw the fangs or make them with clay?" he wonders aloud.

Suddenly there's a loud bang from outside, as if something heavy has just fallen. Some animal makes a screechy, screaming sound. The howl becomes more high-pitched.

"That is definitely a cat!" I say—a very upset, angry, threatening cat.

We jump up and rush to the door. It sounds like a cat fight, but I can hear only one cat screaming. I get to the door first and pull it open, but before I can step out, Maggie grabs my shoulder, holding me back. "Look out!" she cries as a black blur streaks by my feet.